ZUBAAN BOO

THESE HILLS CALL

Temsula Ao has contributed a number of articles on oral tradition, folk songs, myths and cultural traditions of the Ao Nagas in various journals. She has published four collections of poetry and is the author of *Ao-Naga Oral Tradition* (2000). She is a Professor in the Department of English, North Eastern Hill University, Shillong and also Dean, School of Humanities and Education at NEHU.

Zubaan was set up in 2003 as an imprint of Kali for Women, India's first feminist publishing house, whose name is synonymous with women's writing of quality in South Asia. Zubaan has worked to continue and expand on the pioneering list built up by Kali, and many of the books published by us are today considered to be key texts of feminist scholarship.

To mark our tenth anniversary, we are delighted to offer you ten of our classic titles in bold new editions. These are a mixture of original fiction, translations, memoir and non-fiction on a variety of subjects. Each book is unique; each sheds a different light on the world seen through women's eyes, and each holds its place in the world of contemporary women's writing.

Zubaan is proud that these gifted writers have chosen to entrust us with their work, and we are pleased to be able to re-issue these titles to a new readership in the twenty-first century.

Zubaan Classics

Fiction
Temsula Ao *These Hills Called Home*
Kunzang Choden *The Circle of Karma*
Bulbul Sharma, *Eating Women, Telling Tales*
Vandana Singh *The Woman Who Thought She Was a Planet and Other Stories*

Memoir
Baby Halder *A Life Less Ordinary*

Non-fiction
Uma Chakravarti *Rewriting History: The Life and Times of Pandita Ramabai*
Preeti Gill (ed.) *The Peripheral Centre: Voices from the Northeast*
Sharmila Rege *Writing Caste/Writing Gender: Narrating Dalit Women's Testimonios*
Kumkum Sangari and Sudesh Vaid (eds.) *Recasting Women: Essays in Colonial History*
Tanika Sarkar *Words to Win: The Making of a Modern Autobiography*

Note: Since all books are reprints, the bibliographical information they contain on authors has not been updated, and several titles mentioned in them as forthcoming are more than likely to have already appeared.

These Hills Called Home
Stories from a War Zone

TEMSULA AO

zubaan

ZUBAAN
an imprint of Kali for Women
128 B Shahpur Jat, 1st floor
NEW DELHI 110 049
Email: contact@zubaanbooks.com
Website: www.zubaanbooks.com

First published by Zubaan and Penguin Books India 2007
This edition published by Zubaan 2013

10 9 8 7 6 5 4 3 2

ISBN   978 93 81017 97 5

Zubaan is an independent feminist publishing house based in New Delhi with a
strong academic and general list. It was set up as an imprint of India's first feminist
publishing house, Kali for Women, and carries forward Kali's tradition of publishing
world quality books to high editorial and production standards. *Zubaan* means
tongue, voice, language, speech in Hindustani. Zubaan is a non-profit publisher,
working in the areas of the humanities, social sciences, as well as in fiction, general
non-fiction, and books for children and young adults under its Young Zubaan
imprint.

Typset at Sanchauli Image Composers, 28 Nawada Ext., Near Allahabad Bank,
Uttam Nagar, New Delhi 110 059
Printed at Raj Press, R-3 Inderpuri, New Delhi 110 012

For those who know
What we have done
To ourselves

I hear the land cry,
Over and over again
'Let all the dead awaken
And teach the living
How not to die'

Contents

Lest We Forget

Memory is a tricky thing: it picks and chooses what to preserve and what to discard. Sometimes it is the trivial that triggers the process of remembering a great loss. I remember how the memory of my mother's special curry of sun-dried fish used to haunt me long after her death, as though the absence of this exotic dish from the family menu made her death more real than anything else about her. But as I grew into middle age and beyond, it struck me how memories are often sifted through an invisible sieve and selections are made, of both the good and the bad, either to be preserved or discarded. I suppose life has its own inbuilt mechanism of putting its house in order so that human beings can live with a modicum of peace and tranquility.

But what do you do when it comes to someone else's memory and when that memory is of pain and pain alone? Do you brush it aside and say, it does not concern me? And if you can do that, are you the same person that you were, before you learnt of the pain of a fellow human being? I think not, and that is why, in these stories, I have endeavoured to re-visit the lives of those people whose pain has so far gone unmentioned and unacknowledged. Some of them now say that it does not matter, in the same way that some people now say that the holocaust never happened. When these people say that 'it does not matter', they mean that there is an inherent callousness in the human mind that tends to ignore injustice and inhumanity as long as it does not touch one directly. These stories however, are not about 'historical facts'; nor are they about condemnation, justice or justification of the events which raged through the land like a wildfire half a century ago. On the contrary, what the stories are trying to say is that in such conflicts, there are no winners, only victims and the results can be measured only in human terms. For the victims the trauma goes beyond the realm of just the physical maiming and loss of life—their very humanity is assaulted and violated, and the onslaught leaves the survivors scarred both in mind and soul.

Many of the stories in this collection have their genesis in the turbulent years of bloodshed and tears that make up the history of the Nagas from the early fifties of the last century, and their demand for independence from the Indian State. But while the actual struggle remains a backdrop, the thrust of the narratives is to probe how the events of that era have re-structured or even 'revolutionized' the Naga psyche. It was as though a great cataclysmic upheaval threw up many realities for the Nagas within which they are still struggling to settle for a legitimate identity. It was almost like a birth by fire. While some remained untouched by the flames, many others got transformed into beings almost unrecognizable, even to themselves. Nagaland's story of the struggle for self-determination started with high idealism and romantic notions of fervent nationalism, but it somehow got re-written into one of disappointment and disillusionment because it became the very thing it sought to overcome.

A few of the stories in this collection try to capture the ambience of the traditional Naga way of life, which, even for our own youngsters today, is increasingly becoming irrelevant in the face of the 'progress' and 'development' which is only now catching up with the Naga people. The sudden displacement of the young from a placid existence in rural habitats to a world of conflict and confusion in urban settlements is also a fallout of recent Naga history and one that has left them disabled in more way than one.

The inheritors of such a history have a tremendous responsibility to sift through the collective experience and make sense of the impact left by the struggle on their lives. Our racial wisdom has always extolled the virtue of human beings living at peace with themselves and in harmony with nature and with our neighbours. It is only when the Nagas re-embrace and re-write this vision into the fabric of their lives in spite of the compulsions of a fast changing world, can we say that the memories of the turbulent years have served us well.

TEMSULA AO
Shillong

The Jungle Major

In the pre-dawn warmth of togetherness, they made love again with the fervour of lovers meeting after a long absence. They were indeed meeting after a lapse of about five months, but lovers would be a misnomer to describe these two. They were a most mis-matched couple. When their marriage was first announced in the village, people stopped in their tracks, gaped in wonder at the sheer improbability of this match and tsk, tsked, some with disbelief and some in utter disgust at the thought. The girl's father was soundly berated by his clansmen, who said he was lowering the prestige of their clan by agreeing to the match. Why was he condemning his beautiful daughter to life with such a man, they wanted to know.

The relatives', as well as the general public's, indignation over the proposed marriage was due to the immense disparity between not only the outward appearances but also the family positions of the girl and her betrothed. The man was short, dark and had buck teeth. He was a mere driver who knew some mechanics and was employed by a rich man in town to drive a one-ton vehicle called a Dodge, now long gone out of use. He had read only up to class five and could speak some Hindi and a smattering of English picked up in the course of his journeys. He also came from a minor clan in the village.

But the woman. Ah! She was quite another story! She was tall, fair, slim and possessed of the most charming smile. Not only that, she came from a good family and belonged to a major clan.

Her elder brother was studying in the engineering college; her sister was married to a Dobhashi in Mokokchung. Another brother was studying to be a veterinarian doctor. It was rumoured that this beauty had had a string of suitors who courted her but every single one of them eventually drifted away to marry some other village girl much inferior to her in many ways. The villagers were amazed that any sane man would reject such a comely and eligible girl and marry these typically dowdy looking 'village' girls.

But then there it was, the apparent mismatch was on, and the marriage took place in due course. The couple moved to a house of their own, as was the custom, and seemed to be leading a normal life. The man, whose name was Punaba, earned enough to keep his wife in relative comfort. The woman, who was called Khatila, seemed happy and content in her new role as a housewife. Many years passed, but the couple did not have any children. At first the villagers did not pay much attention to this fact. But as it happens in any community, soon rumours began to circulate: the man was either impotent or sterile; or the woman was barren. Some even went to the extent of saying that she did not allow her husband to touch her. Just as the initial announcement of their marriage had produced adverse reactions, now their childless state became the subject of many lewd comments and absurd speculations.

All through this period, the couple, though not unaware of village gossip, ignored the broad hints and snide remarks and appeared to be totally absorbed in each other and their own household. Punaba went on regular trips to nearby villages and after collecting the fares, would go to Mokokchung to give the money to his boss and to receive his salary. Khatila cultivated a small field on the outskirts of the village and grew some vegetables in her kitchen garden. The years of married life seemed to suit her; her beauty remained as fresh as it was during her youth.

It was after a year or so of Khatila's marriage, that the entire land was caught in the new wave of patriotic fervour that swept the imagination of the people and plunged them into a struggle, which many did not even understand. This particular village also became a part of the network, which kept the underground outfit supplied with information, food and occasional arms. The subject of independence became public talk; young people spoke of the exploits of their peers in encounters with government forces and were eager to join the new band of 'patriotic' warriors to liberate their homeland from 'foreign' rule. Some actually disappeared from the village and their names henceforth were spoken only in whispers. Skirmishes were taking place close to the village and the atmosphere within the village became one of fear and mutual suspicion. People returned from their fields much earlier than they used to. It seemed that a pall had descended upon the entire land.

Some villages, to which the underground leaders belonged, were severely punished. The houses were ransacked by the security forces, the grain in their barns was burnt and the people themselves were herded into camps away from the village and kept in virtual imprisonment inside areas fenced in by bamboo stockades. This form of group incarceration was the infamous 'grouping' of villages which the Nagas hated and dreaded even more than bullets. Numerous stories proliferated of women being molested by the security forces and the obstinate ones who refused to give information being severely beaten; not only that, sometimes they would be hung upside down and subjected to unspeakable tortures like chilli powder being rammed into their extremities. But so far, Khatila's village was not touched by any of these horrors as none of their boys who joined the underground movement was of any importance in the eyes of the government and many of them even managed to remain unreported.

One day, Punaba did not return from his usual trip but Khatila did not seem unduly worried by this. A month passed and then another, but there was no sign of this quiet man. When asked about his absence, Khatila replied that he was plying his business in Mokokchung. That sounded plausible, because people there had greater need of a vehicle than the villagers in the area. Before long however, the village grapevine brought news that their very own Punaba had joined the underground army and was, in fact, doing pretty well for himself. It was also reported that strange people visited Khatila with provisions when the adults were away in their fields and disappeared before their return. She became more reclusive and her visits to her parents' home also became less frequent than before.

Not long after the news of Punaba joining the underground army reached the authorities, the government forces came to the village and began questioning the villagers about Punaba. Even Khatila was summoned and asked where her husband was. She replied that she did not know and she did not care whether he came back or not. Judging from the description of the man given by the *gaonbura*, the officer concluded that a beautiful woman like her could not be heartbroken over the disappearance of an insignificant man like Punaba from her life. So they went away after threatening the villagers that if they were withholding vital information about the rebels, they would come back and raze their village to the ground. They even cautioned Khatila that if she was lying to them, she would be punished in a very special way. 'We know how to deal with women like you,' the officer said giving her a lascivious look. In the evening some of the village elders came to her hut and asked her to send word to Punaba not to visit her. Khatila merely nodded her head and meekly replied, 'I shall try.' She knew that even if she could not get in touch with her husband, he would surely come to know about the incident through the underground grapevine. But she had to play the part of a dutiful woman because she knew that in her position she could not afford to antagonise the village authorities in any way.

It was not long before the entire land was engulfed in the flames of conflict between the rebels and the government forces. The oppressive measures adopted by the army to quell the rebellion backfired and even those villages, which were till now not directly involved in the conflict, became more sympathetic towards the underground forces when they heard of the atrocities committed by the armed forces on innocent villagers. By this time, Punaba's fellow villagers were in total sympathy with the so-called rebels and this village became one of the main conduits for supplies and information to them. Punaba sent messengers to Khatila regularly and she knew all that was going on in the underground outfit that her husband was now heading. Because of his age and leadership qualities he rapidly rose in rank and after only three years of service, was made a captain in the rebel army. During these years he even managed to visit his wife several times, even though the visits were short. While he was in the village, lookouts would be posted at strategic points to note the movements of the other army, which patrolled the outskirts of all suspect villages as a routine.

This was one such visit when Punaba had come to see his wife after a gap of five months during which he had been wounded twice and was at the moment recovering from the most recent bullet wound on his right arm. The restful stay with his wife after the arduous and dangerous activities of underground life seemed to be doing wonders for Punaba; he felt healthy and happy for the first time in many months. But all that was soon to be over. That morning, before they could get up from the bed exhausted from the morning's bout of ardent lovemaking, urgent thumps on the bamboo walls were heard, with the whispered warning, 'Sir, sir, wake up, they are almost here, our sentries fell asleep. Run away sir.' Another voice, that of Punaba's orderly joined in, 'Sir, I will hide under the house, throw your gun and uniform to me and I will wait for you on the northern bank of the third well.' The voices melted away with the approaching dawn.

Khatila was in a quandary, what should she do? How could she save her husband, herself and the entire village from the approaching soldiers? She could now hear their voices and the sound of their footsteps on the rocky path leading to their house. For Punaba trying to escape now was out of the question; he would be immediately spotted and shot down like a dog. He would never surrender and she could not lie this time because their small bamboo and thatch house had no hiding place. Though extremely agitated, this woman had enough presence of mind to first bundle up his uniform and gun in a sack and throw it down to the waiting orderly who immediately grabbed it and vanished into the thick jungle. Next, she fished out some of her husband's old clothes and ordered him to get into them, then she smeared his face, hands and feet with ash from the hearth, hid his sandals, ruffled his hair and began shouting at him, 'You no good loafer, what were you doing all day yesterday? There is no water in the house even to wash my face. Run to the well immediately or you will rue the day you were born.' While she was shouting at the top of her voice in this fashion, she was at the same time emptying all the water containers through the bamboo platform at the back. By the time the soldiers reached her house, she was loading the water-carrying basket with the empty containers and showering more abuses at the hapless servant. Someone called out her name and thumped on the door but Khatila continued with her tirade ignoring those standing outside her door. When there was another loud thump she shouted in an irritated voice, 'Who is it now? Don't you see what I am doing?' Taking her own time she opened the door with a loud yawn. 'What do you want?' she growled at the young Captain who looked somewhat surprised at her manner. Whereas he had expected to see a cowering woman, crazy with fear for her husband and herself, he was confronted by a dishevelled but defiant person who displayed no agitation and seemed to be utterly oblivious to any danger. He stood there in confusion; surely the intelligence report was right; that Punaba had come to the village on his periodical visits to his wife and that this was his house. But where was he? He could not have escaped through the tight cordon that was so efficiently put in place by his boys.

Just when he decided to affect a sterner stance, Khatila turned her back on him and began to shout again, 'Hey, where is that lazy so and so? Haven't you gone yet?' The servant, now with the water-carrying basket on his head shuffled out from the bamboo platform at the back and proceeded towards the front door. The young Captain tried to stop him, but Khatila was prepared for this; she said, 'Sahib, no use talking to him, he cannot talk. Besides, don't you see there is no water in the house? What do you want with a servant?' So saying, she gave a shove to Punaba with some more choice abuses and he hurried out of the house and onto the path leading to the third well. Soon he and his small party vanished into the jungle and out of the cordon set up by the soldiers. The Captain did not actually have a clear idea about the person they were looking for, except for the fact that the woman's husband was the wanted man and this house was the target of the search, though several other searches were being carried out by different groups simultaneously in different sectors of the village. The army often employed this tactic to protect their informers, so that in the course of a general search, they would exultantly 'discover' their quarry. Watching the retreating back of the ungainly 'servant', he thought, surely he could not be that person. The young and inexperienced army officer did not realise that the beautiful but simple village woman had thus foiled a meticulously planned 'operation' of the mighty Indian army and that a prized quarry had simply walked away to freedom.

Alone in the house now, she assumed another pose, asking the Captain coyly whether he would like some tea; she could get that much water from her neighbour. The officer was temporarily dazed by Khatila's beauty and would have sat down for tea; but his JCO politely but firmly reminded him, 'Sir, *aor bohut gharka talashi baki hai. Hame chalna hai*'. (Sir there are many more houses to search. We have to move now.) Though slightly irritated, he said '*Thik hai, chalo*' (All right, let's go.) Reluctantly he led the search party away from the house. Only after the entire search party left the village could Khatila relax and she was never more grateful than on that particular morning for the ugliness of her husband which had saved not only them but the entire village. Had he been killed or captured that morning the entire village would have been punished for harbouring a notorious rebel and not informing the government forces about his presence in the village. As had happened to other villages, their barns would have been set on fire, their houses destroyed and the people would have been taken to the 'grouping' areas. But thanks to the audacity of Khatila's ploy, the entire village was saved from such a fate.

Meanwhile the struggle between the rebels and underground forces continued. So did Punaba's periodical visits to see his wife. It was never discovered whether one of their own villagers informed the authorities or the information was supplied by someone else. The escape of Punaba and his party that day was, however, construed differently by the underground bosses and the credit was attributed to his shrewd planning. He continued to serve in the outfit for some three more years and for this particular escape and several other subsequent exploits, he was promoted to the rank of Major in the underground army. When a general cease-fire was announced, Khatila persuaded Punaba to come overground and be with her. She told him that life was becoming too lonesome without him. It also happened to be the period when the government was trying to rehabilitate the 'surrendered' cadres of the underground army, and though he did not possess a regular certificate, Punaba was given a job in the State Transport Department as a mechanic and was posted at Mokokchung.

Years later, the real story of what actually happened on that morning was told, at first only to a few close friends. But by and by this 'exploit' of Punaba, the jungle major, soon became the favourite subject whenever friends dropped in to share a drink in the evenings. Every time the story was recounted, Punaba would look at his wife and ask playfully, 'Aren't you glad that your jungle major is so ugly?' And equally playfully she would answer, 'So, where is the water I sent you to fetch that day?'

Soaba

No one really knew who his parents were or which village he came from. He grew up as the town orphan living on people's charity, often doing odd jobs like fetching water and splitting wood in various households. Even though many people tried to domesticate and keep him as their permanent unpaid servant, he would not stay in one place for more than a week or so. The longest that he stayed in one fixed 'place' was the time when people saw him travelling on a P.W.D. truck with the driver for several weeks. But there was no pattern in the comings and goings of this peculiar boy; he came and went as he pleased. No one could do anything about his wandering from household to household; the townspeople simply accepted him as he was and gave him food and shelter when he appeared at their doorstep.

Imtimoa was his name, although no one knew who gave him that name. People mostly referred to him as Soaba, which means 'idiot' in the Ao language. Soaba was obviously slow in the head and seldom spoke coherently. His vocabulary consisted of simple sentences like 'I am hungry', 'Give me more' and at times loud screams of 'No, don't do that'. But, more often than not, he expressed his feelings with gestures or grunts. Though this boy was totally unaware of any reality except hunger and thirst and shelter from the cold and rain, he was destined to be caught up in the whirlwind sweeping through the land and creating havoc in people's lives.

It was the late fifties and new happenings in the land were overturning the even tenor of people's lives. Though they had been living in small townships, their rural and traditional outlook on life still dominated the environment. These were people who had migrated to the townships as petty clerks in government offices, teachers in the various schools and also as small-scale traders who preferred urban life to a life of hard work and meagre returns in the villages. Unlike the homogenous population of villages, the citizens of these new towns belonged to all the tribes of Nagaland. One particular group, of course, would outnumber the others purely on geographical factors. For example, a town like Mokokchung would obviously have more Aos than Angamis or Semas because the town is in the Ao territory. Such towns also had many 'outsiders': Assamese or Bengali doctors or teachers, Marwari and Bihari traders, Nepali settlers, whose forefathers had fought with the British army and were given land to settle down. Slowly but steadily, a new environment was emerging and overtaking the old ways, and youngsters growing up in such places began to think of themselves as the new generation.

These young people were caught, as it were, at the crossroads of Naga history. The wave of dissidence and open rebellion was heady wine for many of them and they abandoned family, school careers and even permanent jobs to join the band of nationalists to liberate the homeland from forces, which they believed, were inimical to their aspirations to be counted among the free nations of the world. It was however not only the people from the urban areas who joined these forces. Through a method not dissimilar to 'conscription' based on clans, many rural adults had to abandon family and fieldwork and were inducted into the 'underground' army of freedom fighters.

It was at this stage that a new vocabulary also began to creep into the everyday language of the people. Words like convoy, grouping, curfew and 'situation' began to acquire sinister dimensions as a result of the conflict taking place between the government and underground armies. Convoys meant the massive deployment of army personnel to various strategic areas;

convoys were also the only permitted mode of travel for people who had to go to different places on official or personal errands. Travelling with long lines of huge and unwieldy army vehicles meant slow progress because when one vehicle stopped, every other vehicle had to do so too. The roads were dusty, unmetalled and the alignments were haphazard; some were cut into the sheer rock face of the hills with very little space for negotiating sharp bends. Many accidents took place, especially when visibility was poor due to the constant umbrella of fog enveloping the hills. On clear days, it was the dust churned out by the vehicle in front, which hampered visibility and slowed progress. These convoys were also frequently the targets of ambushes from the other side, often resulting in not only army but civilian casualties as well. The word 'grouping' had a much more sinister implication; it meant that whole villages would be dislodged from their ancestral sites and herded into new ones, making it more convenient for the security forces to guard them day and night. The harrowing tales of people who experienced such forced migrations are not fully known and some of the accounts have died with the unfortunate ones who did not survive the intense physical and mental torture meted out to them. If there was one single factor, which further alienated the Nagas, it was this form of punishing 'errant' villages. It was the most humiliating insult that was inflicted on the Naga psyche by forcibly uprooting them from the soil of their origin and being, and confining them in an alien environment, denying them access to their fields, restricting them from their routine activities and most importantly, demonstrating to them that the 'freedom' they enjoyed could so easily be robbed at gunpoint by the 'invading' army. Curfew, a word that did not exist in the people's vocabulary, became a dreaded fact of life for people living in the towns. A word like 'situation' is a perfectly innocent one, but in the context of the underground movement, it acquired a singular meaning: it referred only to the fall-out of the struggle between the two opposing forces.

But the 'fight' taking place in the jungles did not reflect the conflict of interests that was eating into the moral fabric of a society where friendship and loyalty were the casualties. The new breed of the disgruntled did not all take up arms; they became the disquieting elements in the power struggle between the two warring groups. This environment was created by the government; they needed a band of die-hards who would be their 'extra arms' beyond the law and civil rights and who would also 'guide' their forces who were so pitiably uninformed not only about the terrain on which they were fighting and dying, but also about a bunch of people so alien to them that for all they knew, they could have come from a different planet! So a band of self-seeking entrepreneurs entered the arena of this strange warfare. They were designated as Home Guards by the government, ostensibly formed for civil defense duties but in the town of Mokokchung, there was a unit of this force which came to be known as the 'flying squad', led by a notorious ex-cop reputed to be the perpetrator of several heinous crimes. This band was equipped with vehicles as well as guns, and was given free rations of rum to boot. They zoomed around town in these conveyances of notoriety intimidating and harassing the public at will, often settling old scores with rivals whom they would not have dared to challenge under normal circumstances. What follows is the story of a most unlikely person who attached himself to this group because of his fascination with the vehicles in which they travelled around the town.

Since the day Soaba saw a squad vehicle scream past him on the street, he became obsessed with them. He would watch in wide-eyed wonder as far as he could see and was often seen running after the speeding vehicles. In his wanderings across town, one day he chanced to see such a vehicle parked in the compound of the leader and from that day onwards he hovered near the fence around it. Once or twice, a guard shooed him off, only to find him standing in another spot close to the fence. When this went on for a few days, the wife came out one day and beckoned to him with a plate of rice. He did not hesitate even for a moment, jumped over the fence and, grabbing the plate, devoured the contents hungrily. From that day onwards, Soaba became a fixture in the household from which he would not have moved but for the tragedy, which ended his short sojourn there.

In the meantime, the fortunes of the leader of this squad seemed to be changing dramatically. His name was Imlichuba but he preferred to be called Boss, so everyone called him Boss. He was fast becoming a dreaded figure in the new hierarchy being created by the government forces to counter the influence of the rebel movement. His image as an ally of the government was increasingly enhanced because of his unquestioned authority over people suspected of subversive activities or those suspected of being agents of the underground outfit. Army bigwigs and senior administrative officers visited his house regularly, which was now renovated with new fixtures and a fresh coat of paint. It was now more securely fenced in with regular guards at the two gates. His personal appearance too began to change; he started wearing new and fashionable clothes and flashy rings on his fingers. Neighbours often saw parcels and crates being delivered through the back gate after dark. It was also after dark that his other visitors, the ones with dark coats or heavy blankets and with head and face covered by mufflers, would enter through the back gate for their business. It soon became a pattern that a day or two after such a visit, there would be a raid in a nearby village or even in the town itself and the army would arrest suspected collaborators. Sometimes, a few of these arrested persons would be brought to the Boss's house and left there for 'proper interrogation' by him and his boys. Often, screams and groans emanating from the depths of this house, could be heard above the loud music blaring out from the only record player in town owned by Boss. No one knew what eventually happened to these people; if some survived the tortures, they would either surface in the civil hospital or the local jail. Quite a few were never seen again. Though the beatings and tortures were common knowledge, people were scared to open their mouths much less admit they had heard or seen something they shouldn't have.

Soaba, who now slept in a small room in the wood shed, saw the comings and goings through a hole in the bamboo wall and heard the agonised screams of the detainees. Through the haze in his mind he sensed that something bad was happening in this house. After a week or so, one morning he tried to go out of the gate but a guard saw him and called him back to split some wood. After he finished the chore, he was given his meal and somehow Soaba forgot that he had wanted to go out at all and settled down to his usual routine of watching the vehicles come and go or listening to the songs coming out of a box in the house. In all this while no one spoke to him except to tell him to chop wood or fetch things for the other workers in the household. Nor did he try to say anything to anyone. Then one day he happened to hear Boss screaming at someone in a loud voice. He did not understand what was being said but he caught a phrase being shouted repeatedly. Boss was calling someone 'stupid bastard', which to Soaba's unschooled ears sounded like 'supiba' and from that moment on he wanted to be called Supiba instead of Soaba, because even to his simple mind, Supiba somehow sounded better than Soaba. He tried to tell the people around him that he wanted to be called Supiba instead of Soaba. At first they did not understand what he was trying to say; but he kept on pointing to himself and saying Supiba in the garbled way that he spoke. When someone from inside the house called out Soaba, the boy began to scream Supiba, Supiba. Only then did they understand what he wanted from them and from that time on they called him Supiba in deference to a simple mind, which in some mysterious way had sensed that there was something bad about the name Soaba that was tagged on to him.

Boss's wife, who was called Imtila, was basically a simple woman and would have loved to continue being a normal housewife, looking after her husband and children. But her husband's changed fortunes compelled her to set aside her hitherto sedate and domesticated lifestyle and adopt one more in keeping with her husband's new status. While entertaining, she was required to wear the expensive clothes and jewellery that Boss bought for her She was expected to circulate among the strangers who came to the parties and be the amiable hostess. He declared that she could not go out anywhere without a bodyguard and her friends or relatives could not come to the house freely like before. Gradually she became a prisoner of her husband's notoriety because her friends and relatives, sensing her discomfiture when they called on her a few times, began to stay away and even when the husband invited them on important occasions, they bluntly refused to come.

The coming of the boy, now called Supiba, therefore was a welcome diversion for the lonely woman. She would go out to the shed where he stayed and watch his simple-minded activities like rolling on the ground or playing with sticks and stones all by himself. Seeing how dirty he was, one day she ordered her servants to give him a proper bath and bought him new clothes to wear instead of the rags he was always seen in. He was given a free run of the compound but was not allowed inside the house. By and by his section of the wood shed was cleaned up and a new cot was put in on her orders. She always enquired whether Supiba had been given his meal or not. This transference of affection to the idiot began to have a strange effect on Boss's wife; for the first time in her life she began to think for herself and assess the true nature of her husband's work. When he was first inducted to the new force, she was happy, thinking that at last there was going to be some discipline and order in his life and work. But as time went by, it became clear that the opposite was happening; he was surrounded by a bunch of savages in his squad, some of whom were hardened criminals let loose by the authorities to carry out their despicable designs. Some were deserters from the underground army who had left the hard life of the jungle and, lured by easy money and booze, had joined the new outfit. These people seemed to infest her environment. She could no longer call her home her personal domain, there was no peace and quiet for her or the children because her husband's lackeys seemed to be everywhere, inside the house, in the compound and some even had the audacity to enter their bedroom on the pretext of giving a message to Boss. She avoided them when they started drinking at night because then they became more abusive in language and violent in temper. And if there happened to be any detainees undergoing 'interrogation', they bore the brunt of their drunken savagery. Then the night would erupt with the unearthly screams and cries of the victims and even though the record player did its best to muffle the sounds, the walls of the house seemed to reverberate with their agony; and the poor woman with this knowledge in her heart would writhe in an agony of helplessness. Sometimes she would even run to the bathroom and vomit whatever little food she had eaten.

Boss was becoming impossible to live with; he had no time for his wife or children now, they were becoming more like receding blurs than real persons in his turbulent life. In his own way, he, too, sensed that his wife had gone away from the sanctuary of their relationship and had retreated into a world where he had no place. But he was so drunk with his own power, which had deadened his human spirit, that he became insensitive to this inner voice. Even the outward appearance of the marital relationship snapped when Imtila removed herself from his presence and took to sleeping in a different room. He soon lost all physical desire, not only for her but also for any other woman. But out of a perverse sense of proving his manhood, he would order women to be brought to the house for his pleasure. On these occasions however, he discovered that he could not find the energy or the desire to make love to them. The ones who went away tamely were rewarded but the bolder and experienced ones who tried either to talk lightly of middle-aged men and impotency or tried to revive his flagging organ were mercilessly beaten and dumped outside the gate by his guards.

Though Imtila was aware of these nocturnal visits to her husband's bedside and what happened to many of the women who had been either lured by the promise of money and a good time or were forcibly brought to him, she found that she no longer cared and felt only a deep sympathy for the unfortunate women. The townspeople soon came to know about this aspect of Boss's deteriorating life-style and word went out to all families with young girls to keep a strict vigil over their daughters, especially after nightfall. Boss would frequently invite his army pals and government officials for a party in his house. At such times, Supiba would become restless and would even refuse to eat. Instead, he would sit in a corner of the compound and whimper. He had somehow come to associate big crowds and loud music with something bad, either happening at that very moment or about to happen. On such nights, the visitors would bring their own female escorts and drink and dance late into the night. Imtila at first was compelled to mingle with the guests at least for a short while, but as the estrangement between husband and wife grew, she ceased to do even that. On party nights now she would lock herself in her room, refusing even the food and drink that her maid brought for her.

On a particular night when the guest list seemed to be larger than usual and there was much going in and going out throughout the day, Supiba managed to sneak into the kitchen under cover of darkness and hide himself in the small pantry, which was stocked with provisions for the party. That evening, Imtila made a rare visit to the pantry to look for something and discovered the boy crouched in a corner. At first she seemed angry, and was about to scold him but when she saw the forlorn and frightened look on his face, she restrained herself and instead motioning to him to be quiet and covering him with her shawl, managed to take him into the room she now occupied. There she pushed him under the bed and held her finger to her lips to tell him that he should keep quiet. As usual, the party got on its way and as the night progressed, the loud laughter and hysterical screams of the girls rang out from all directions to indicate that things were getting out of control. Once in a while one of the drunken men would discharge his gun in the air and for a few seconds there would be complete silence. But soon it would be followed by more raucous laughter as the party continued its wild course.

Boss's excessive drinking and increasingly wild behaviour was beginning to irk his handlers. Whereas once he had been their special man to carry out their shadowy operations discreetly, he had now become more of a liability than an asset. The powers that had at one time released or reined in the leash on him at will, found it almost impossible to keep him in check. He now seemed to be running away with the leash, pulling them along and threatening to expose the sinister abuses perpetrated by his gang on innocent civilians at their behest. So they decided to put a damper on his drunken escapades by putting fear in his mind; fear for his life. Earlier in the day, a messenger from Brigade Headquarter had come to the house with cases of rum and whiskey and also a message from the Brigade Major warning him of a possible attempt on his life from people in his own squad. But instead of feeling intimidated, Boss became defiant and even more belligerent. The party was turning out to be more boisterous than usual and Boss seemed to be on a special high. One moment he would regale the gathering with bawdy jokes and the crowd would burst into raucous laughter and then, suddenly, his mood would change and he would begin shouting about traitors and what he was going to do to these dogs. Someone, drunkenly breaking into a Hindi song, would somehow interrupt the momentary silence induced by the tirade and the party would continue. Tonight the supply of liquor seemed to be unlimited and the revellers paid little attention to Boss's drunken outbursts. But around midnight, one of Boss's bodyguards was seen whispering something into his ear. Boss jumped up in a rage and shouted, 'There is a traitor in this house tonight who has come to kill me. We will search every person and every room until we find him and show what happens to traitors.' All activity stopped, each person was looking at the other as if seeing him or her for the first time. It was one of those moments when temporary sobriety is restored by extreme fear. People seemed to sag in their seats if they were sitting and if standing, they somehow seemed to shrivel in their places. In the deathly silence that followed this declaration, only the faint shrill of a pressure cooker could be heard from the region of the kitchen.

In the meantime, Supiba was feeling cramped under Imtila's bed. He had lain there since early evening. So he had crawled out when she had gone to the bathroom and looking into a drawer of the dressing table, saw what he thought was a toy, he had seen those objects in the hands of the children playing in the compound. He went forward to pick it up, when suddenly the door to the room was kicked open and Boss was standing there swaying unsteadily on drunken legs. Supiba, like a cornered animal began to whimper. Hearing the commotion, Imtila opened the door of the bathroom gingerly and stopped in mid-track at what she saw: Boss, taking deliberate aim was about to shoot Supiba in the head, execution style. She screamed and said, 'Wait, it is only Soaba, don't shoot'. She made as if to lunge at her husband at which point Boss redirected his aim at Imtila's heart, hissing 'traitor' through grated teeth. It was then that Supiba sprang into action. Growling like a fierce animal he tried to jump at Boss, putting himself in the range of the gun's aim and shielding Imtila. 'Boss, Boss', someone was trying to say something to him but he was beyond all human reasoning; he was still hissing the word traitor out of his foaming mouth. Even as Supiba tried to signal something with his hand, which still clutched the gun, the drunken figure discharged his weapon straight into his heart. With a piercing cry of anguish, Imtila rushed to the body of the fallen idiot crying over and over again, 'Oh my poor boy, were you born for this? Why did I let you come into this evil place?' She was disconsolate, weeping and muttering these words again and again in a monotonous dirge-like tone. A stupefied Boss was led away by his bodyguards into the din of the raucous party, which continued as if nothing had happened.

The next day, the townspeople heard that Supiba had died in an accident while playing with a gun left near him by a careless guard. No one dared ask who that irresponsible wretch was. They also heard that Imtila had washed his body herself and dressed him in Boss's best suit before it was put in the coffin. The actual circumstances of the death were never fully investigated nor talked about and this poor idiot boy who chanced to be in this malfeasant circle created by Boss and his cohorts was buried in a far corner of the town cemetery, with only the reluctant pastor and a grieving Imtila accompanying the pallbearers. After the funeral, Imtila locked herself in her room and stayed there for three days, refusing to open it to anyone except her maid who brought her food. On the fourth day she came out and ordered the servants to remove all signs of Soaba's existence from the compound. The cot, piled high with his old clothes, was taken to a far corner of the garden and burnt. It was as though she was obliterating a painful chapter of her own life through this ritual.

Soon the household appeared to resume its old routine; Boss still strutted around, his bodyguards at his side even inside the compound. He would still ride out in the jeep escorted by his lackeys. He still drank heavily, but the liquor now had a different effect on him. Instead of making him boisterous and even aggressive, he became morose. Some other imperceptible changes were also beginning to creep into the routine of the household. The parties became less frequent and eventually stopped. Fewer people visited Boss after the incident, some of his trusted lieutenants asked for leave to go and visit 'ailing' relatives and quite a few of them did not return. The music from the record player stopped and even the squad vehicles plied less on the town roads.

Imtila began to notice the effects of these changes on the behaviour of her estranged husband. He became listless and disinterested in anything around him; it was as if a vital string had snapped in his evil genius when he pulled the trigger that night. Like a man awakened from a long trance Boss stole around the house as if he was trying to familiarise himself with a new environment. But every now and then he would go on a drinking binge lasting for days, become abusive and start shouting at everyone; then suddenly he would collapse in a drunken heap muttering to himself, 'Oh you idiot, you idiot'. Though Imtila was indifferent at first, she gradually found she could no longer ignore the behavioural changes in her husband, and his growing depression, which was threatening to destroy his sanity. So she quietly moved back into their old bedroom and began to make overtures of reconciliation to this man who seemed to have diminished from his former evil self into a whimpering helpless child. She tried to pick up the broken pieces of their former life and create a new order from the pathetic remains. It was not an easy task but she persevered because the alternative was too frightening to contemplate.

It must, however, be said that the public persona of Boss did continue to harass people and haunt their minds because the government saw to it that he did not altogether lose his former standing as the commander of the dreaded squad. They visited his house occasionally and sent him gifts. On certain days he would even dress up in his squad uniform and, accompanied by a few of his faithful boys, drive round the town but whoever saw him on these occasions sensed that the sting had gone out of him because he would sit stone-like, staring straight ahead as if he was in a trance. In the old days he would stand in the jeep, brandishing his gun, his face flushed with drink and mouth crimson with *paan,* he would let out loud whoops of derision as the townspeople scampered to get out of the way of the speeding vehicles. Recalling the earlier spectacle and watching the present parody, some even went to the extent of saying that he now looked definitely shrunken in size. The realisation soon dawned on the people that what had at one time loomed over the town as a huge and menacing blot was fast becoming a mere smudge on the horizon.

In his heyday, Boss loved to dress up in three-piece suits for his parties and it was rumoured that he never wore a suit more than once. People often wondered aloud how many suits he owned if that rumour was true. Now that his exploits were becoming a thing of the turbulent past, people's attention turned to his present personal circumstances. And on the question of his clothes, they wondered if Boss ever found out what happened to his best suit. The speculations continued and no one could say for sure whether he ever found out that it was buried with Soaba. But curiosity about Boss never ceased and by and by they learned from 'reliable' sources within his household that after the 'sad accident' in his house when the town idiot was killed, Boss was never seen in a suit again.

Thus ended the tragic tale of Soaba, who, like a bewildered animal, had strayed out of his natural habitat into a maze that simply swallowed him up. The magic of Boss' fast cars had drawn him into a world where violence was the order of the day and which eventually claimed his life. There was no one to mourn his death except a heart-wounded woman who was desperately trying to cling on to humanity amidst the chaos that had engulfed her world. In spite of the wretchedness of her own life, she had tried to give him a certain measure of love, protection and care. But all her concern and affectionate care proved inadequate when it came to protecting him from the senseless death brought on him by her own husband.

The Last Song

It seemed the little girl was born to sing. Her mother often recalled that when she was a baby, she would carry her piggyback to community singing events on festival days. As soon as the singers took up a tune and gradually when their collective voices began to swell in volume and harmony, her daughter would twist herself this way and that and start singing her own version of the song, mostly consisting of loud shrieks and screams. Though amusing at first, her daughter's antics irritated the spectators and the singers as well, and often, she had to withdraw from the gathering in embarrassment. What the mother considered unreasonable behaviour in a child barely a year old, was actually the first indication of the singing genius that she had given birth to.

When Apenyo, as the little girl was called, could walk and talk a little, her mother would take her to church on Sundays because she could not be left alone at home. On other days she was left in the care of her grandmother when the mother went to the fields; but on this day there was no one to take care of her as everyone went to church. When the congregation sang together Apenyo would also join, though her little screams were not quite audible because of the group singing. But whenever there was a special number, trouble would begin; Apenyo would try to sing along, much to the embarrassment of the mother. After two or three such mortifying Sunday outings, the mother stopped going to church altogether until Apenyo became older and learnt how to behave.

At home too, Apenyo never kept quiet; she hummed or made up silly songs to sing by herself, which annoyed her mother at times but most often made her become pensive. She was by now convinced that her daughter had inherited her love of singing from her father who had died so unexpectedly away from home. The father, whose name was Zhamben, was a gifted singer both of traditional folk songs as well as of Christian hymns at church. Naga traditional songs consist of polyphonic notes and harmonising is the dominant feature of such community singing. Perhaps because of his experience and expertise in folk songs, Zhamben picked up the new tunes of hymns quite easily and soon became the lead male voice in the church choir. He was a schoolteacher in the village and at the time of his death was undergoing a teacher-training course in a town in Assam. He was suddenly taken ill and by the time the news reached the village, he was already dead. While his relatives were preparing to go and visit him, his friends from the training school brought his dead body home. Apenyo was only nine months old then. From that time on, it was a lonely struggle for the mother, trying to cultivate a field and bring up a small child on her own. With occasional help from her in-laws and her own relatives, the widow, called Libeni, was slowly building a future for her daughter and herself. Many of the relatives told her to get married again so that she and little Apenyo would have a man to protect and look after them. But Libeni would not listen and when they repeatedly told her to think about it seriously, she asked them never to bring up the subject again. So mother and daughter lived alone and survived mainly on what was grown in the field.

At the village school Apenyo did well and became the star pupil. When she was old enough to help her mother in spreading the thread on the loom, she would sit nearby and watch her weave the colourful shawls, which would be sold to bring in additional income. Libeni had the reputation of being one of the best weavers in the village and her shawls were in great demand.

By and by Apenyo too learned the art from her mother and became an excellent weaver like her. In the meantime, her love for singing too was growing. People soon realized that not only did she love to sing but also that Apenyo had an exquisite singing voice. She was inducted into the church choir where she soon became the lead soprano. Every time the choir sang it was her voice that made even the commonest song sound heavenly. Along with her singing voice, her beauty also blossomed as Apenyo approached her eighteenth birthday. Her natural beauty seemed to be enhanced by her enchanting voice, which earned her the nickname 'singing beauty' in the village. Libeni's joy knew no bounds. She was happy that all those years of loneliness and hardship were well rewarded by God through her beautiful and talented daughter.

One particular year, the villagers were in an especially expectant mood because there was a big event coming up in the village church in about six months time: the dedication of the new church building. Every member of the church had contributed towards the building fund by donating in cash and kind and it had taken them nearly three years to complete the new structure of tin roof and wooden frames to replace the old one of bamboo and thatch. In every household the womenfolk were planning new clothes for the family, brand new shawls for the men and new skirts or 'lungis' for the women. The whole village was being spruced up for the occasion as some eminent pastors from neighbouring villages were being invited for the dedication service. Pigs earmarked for the feast were given special food to fatten them up. The service was planned for the first week of December, which would ensure that harvesting of the fields would be over and the special celebration would not interfere with the normal Christmas celebrations of the church. The villagers began the preparations with great enthusiasm, often joking among themselves that this year they would have a double Christmas!

These were, however, troubled times for the Nagas. The Independence movement was gaining momentum by the day and even the remotest villages were getting involved, if not directly in terms of their members joining the underground army, then certainly by paying 'taxes' to the underground 'government'. This particular village was no different. They had been compelled to pay their dues every year, the amount calculated on the number of households in the village. Curiously enough, the collections would be made just before the Christmas holidays, perhaps because travel for the collectors was easier through the winter forests or perhaps they too wanted to celebrate Christmas! In any case, the villagers were prepared for the annual visit from their brethren of the forests and the transaction was carried out without a hitch.

But this year, it was not as simple as in previous years. A recent raid of an underground hideout yielded records of all such collections of the area and the government forces were determined to 'teach' all those villages the consequences of 'supporting' the rebel cause by paying the 'taxes'. Unknown to them, a sinister plan was being hatched by the forces to demonstrate to the entire Naga people what happens when you 'betray' your own government. It was decided that the army would go to this particular village on the day when they were dedicating the new church building and arrest all the leaders for their 'crime' of paying taxes to the underground forces.

In the meanwhile, the villagers caught up in the hectic activities prior to the appointed day, a Sunday, were happily busy in tidying up their own households, especially the ones where the guests would be lodged. The dedication Sunday dawned bright and cool, it was December after all, and every villager, attired in his or her best, assembled in front of the new church, which was on the same site as the old one. The villagers were undecided about what to do with the old one still standing near the new one. They had postponed any decision until after the dedication. That morning the choir was standing together in the front porch of the new church to lead the congregation in the singing before the formal inauguration, after which they would enter the new building. Apenyo, the lead singer, was standing in the middle of the front row, looking resplendent in her new lungi and shawl. She was going to perform solo on the occasion after the group song of the choir. As the pastor led the congregation in the invocatory prayer, a hush fell on the crowd as though in great expectation: the choir would sing their first number after the prayer. As the song the crowd was waiting to hear began, there was the sound of gunfire in the distance; it was an ominous sound which meant that the army would certainly disrupt the festivities. But the choir sang on unfazed, though uneasy shuffles could be heard from among the crowd. The pastor too began to look worried; he turned to a deacon and seemed to be consulting with about something. Just as the singing subsided, another sound reverberated throughout the length and breath of the village: a frightened Dobashi, with fear and trembling in his voice was telling the people to stay where they were and not to attempt to run away or fight. There was a stunned silence and the congregation froze in their places unable to believe that their dedication Sunday was going to be desecrated by the arrogant Indian army.

Very soon the approaching soldiers surrounded the crowd, and the pastor was commanded to come forward and identify himself along with the *gaonburas*. But before they could do anything, Apenyo burst into her solo number, and not to be outdone by the bravery or foolishness of this young girl, and not wishing to leave her thus exposed, the entire choir burst into song. The soldiers were incensed; it was an act of open defiance and proper retaliation had to be made. They pushed and shoved the pastor and the gaonburas, prodding them with the butts of their guns towards the waiting jeeps below the steps of the church. Some of the villagers tried to argue with the soldiers and they too were kicked and assaulted. There was a feeble attempt by the accompanying Dobashi to restore some semblance of order but no one was listening to him and the crowd, by now overcome by fear and anger, began to disperse in every direction. Some members of the choir left their singing and were seen trying to run away to safety. Only Apenyo stood her ground. She sang on, oblivious of the situation as if an unseen presence was guiding her. Her mother, standing with the congregation, saw her daughter singing her heart out as if to withstand the might of the guns with her voice raised to God in heaven. She called out to her to stop but Apenyo did not seem to hear or see anything. In desperation, Libeni rushed forward to pull her daughter away but the leader of the army was quicker. He grabbed Apenyo by the hair and with a bemused look on his face dragged her away from the crowd towards the old church building. All this while, the girl was heard singing the chorus of her song over and over again.

There was chaos everywhere. Villagers trying to flee the scene were either shot at or kicked and clubbed by the soldiers who seemed to be everywhere. The pastor and the gaonburas were tied up securely for transportation to army headquarters and whatever fate awaited them there. More people were seen running away desperately, some seeking security in the old church and some even entered the new one hoping that at least the house of God would offer them safety from the soldiers. Libeni was now frantic. Calling out her daughter's name loudly, she began to search for her in the direction where she was last seen being dragged away by the leader. When she came upon the scene at last, what she saw turned her stomach: the young Captain was raping Apenyo while a few other soldiers were watching the act and seemed to be waiting for their turn. The mother, crazed by what she was witnessing, rushed forward with an animal-like growl as if to haul the man off her daughter's body but a soldier grabbed her and pinned her down on the ground. He too began to unzip his trousers and when Libeni realised what would follow next, she spat on the soldier's face and tried to twist herself free of his grasp. But this only further aroused him; he bashed her head on the hard ground several times knocking her unconscious and raped her limp body, using the woman's new lungi afterwards, which he had flung aside, to wipe himself. The small band of soldiers then took their turn, even though by the time the fourth one mounted, the woman was already dead. Apenyo, though terribly bruised and dazed by what was happening to her was still alive, though barely so. Some of the villagers who had entered the old church saw what happened to mother and daughter and after the soldiers were seen going towards the village square, came out to help them. As they were trying to lift the limp bodies, the Captain happened to look back and seeing that there were witnesses to their despicable act, turned to his soldiers and ordered them to open fire on the people who were now lifting up the bodies of the two women. Amid screams and yells the bodies were dropped as the helpless villagers once again tried to seek shelter inside the church.

Returning towards the scene of their recent orgy, the Captain saw the grotesque figures of the two women, both dead. He shouted an order to his men to dump them on the porch of the old church. He then ordered them to take positions around the church and at his signal they emptied their guns into the building. The cries of the wounded and the dying inside the church proved that even the house of God could not provide them security and save them from the bullets of the crazed soldiers. In the distance too, similar atrocities were taking place. But the savagery was not over yet. Seeing that it would be a waste of time and bullets to kill off all the witnesses inside the church, the order was given to set it on fire. Yelling at the top of his voice, the Captain now appeared to have gone mad. He snatched the box of matches from his Adjutant and set to work. But his hands were shaking; he thought that he could still hear the tune the young girl was humming as he was ramming himself into her virgin body, while all throughout, the girl's unseeing eyes were fixed on his face. He slumped down on the ground and the soldiers made as if to move away, but with renewed anger he once again gave the order and the old church soon burst into flames reducing the dead and the dying into an unrecognizable black mass. The new church too, standing not so far from the old one, caught the blaze and was badly damaged. Elsewhere in the village, the granaries were the first to go up in flames. The wind carried burning chunks from these structures and scattered them amidst the clusters of houses, which too burnt to the ground.

By the time the marauding soldiers left the village with their prisoners, it was dark and to compound the misery it rained the whole night. It was impossible to ascertain how many men and women were missing apart from the pastor and the four gaonburas. Mercifully, the visiting pastors were left alone when it became known that they did not belong to this village. But they were ordered to leave immediately and threatened in no uncertain terms that if they carried the news of what had happened here, their own villages would suffer the same fate. The search for the still missing persons began only the next morning. They found out that among the missing persons were Apenyo and her mother. When a general tally was taken, it was discovered that many villagers sustained bullet wounds as well as injuries from severe beatings. Also, six members of the choir were not accounted for. An old woman whose house was quite close to the church site told the search party that she saw some people running towards the old church.

When the villagers arrived at the burnt-out site of the old church building, their worst suspicions were confirmed. Among the rain-drenched ashes of the old church they found masses of human bones washed clean by the night's rain. And on what was once the porch of the old church, they found a separate mass and through a twist of fate a piece of Apenyo's new shawl was found, still intact beneath the pile of charred bones. Mother and daughter lay together in that pile. The villagers gathered all the bones of the six choir members and put them in a common coffin but those of the mother and daughter, they put in a separate one. After a sombre and song-less funeral service, the question arose as to where to bury them. Though the whole village had embraced Christianity long ago, some of the old superstitions and traditions had not been totally abandoned. The deaths of these unfortunate people were considered to be from unnatural causes and according to tradition they could not be buried in the village graveyard, Christianity or no Christianity. Some younger ones protested, 'How can you say that? They were members of our church and sang in the choir'. The old ones countered this by saying, 'So what, we are still Nagas aren't we? And for us some things never change'. The debate went on for some time until a sort of compromise was reached: they would be buried just outside the boundary of the graveyard to show that their fellow villagers had not abandoned their remains to a remote forest site. But there was a stipulation: no headstones would be erected for any of them.

Today these gravesites are two tiny grassy knolls on the perimeter of the village graveyard and if one is not familiar with the history of the village, particularly about what happened on that dreadful Sunday thirty odd years ago, one can easily miss these two mounds trying to stay above ground level. The earth may one day swallow them up or rip them open to reveal the charred bones. No one knows what will happen to these graves without headstones or even to those with elaborately decorated concrete structures inside the hallowed ground of the proper graveyard, housing masses of bones of those who died 'natural' deaths. But the story of what happened to the ones beneath the grassy knolls without the headstones, especially of the young girl whose last song died with her last breath, lived on in the souls of those who survived the darkest day of the village.

And what about the Captain and his band of rapists who thought that they had burnt all the evidence of their crime? No one knows for sure. But the underground network, which seems able to ferret out the deadliest of secrets, especially about perpetrators of exceptional cruelty on innocent villagers, managed not only to piece together the events of that black Sunday, but also to ascertain the identity of the Captain. After several years of often frustrating intelligence gathering, he was traced to a military hospital in a big city where he was being kept in a maximum-security cell of an insane asylum.

P.S. It is a cold night in December and in a remote village, an old storyteller is sitting by the hearth-fire with a group of students who have come home for the winter holidays. They love visiting her to listen to her stories, but tonight granny is not her usual chirpy self; she looks much older and seems to be agitated over something. One of the boys asks her whether she is not feeling well and tells her that if so, they can come back another night. But instead of answering the question, the old woman starts talking and tells them that on certain nights a peculiar wind blows through the village, which seems to start from the region of the graveyard and which sounds like a hymn. She also tells them that tonight is that kind of a night. At first the youngsters are skeptical and tell her that they cannot hear anything and that such things are not possible, but the old woman rebukes them by saying that they are not paying attention to what is happening around them. She tells them that youngsters of today have forgotten how to listen to the voice of the earth and the wind. They feel chastised and make a show of straining their ears to listen more attentively and to their utter surprise, they hear the beginning of a low hum in the distance. They listen for some time and tell her, almost in triumph, that they can hear only an eerie sound. 'No', the storyteller almost shouts, 'Listen carefully. Tonight is the anniversary of that dreadful Sunday'. There is a death-like silence in the room and some of them begin to look uneasy because they too had heard vague rumours of army atrocities that took place in the village on a Sunday long before they were born. Storyteller and audience strain to listen more attentively and suddenly a strange thing happens: as the wind whirls past the house, it increases in volume and for the briefest of moments seems to hover above the house. Then it resumes its whirling as though hurrying away to other regions beyond human habitation. The young people are stunned because they hear the new element in the volume and a certain uncanny lilt lingers on in the wake of its departure. The old woman jumps up from her seat and looking at each one in turn asks, 'You heard it, didn't you? Didn't I tell you? It was Apenyo's last song' and she hums a tune softly, almost to herself. The youngsters cannot deny that they heard the note but are puzzled because they do not know what she is talking about. As the old woman stands apart humming the tune, they look at her with wonder. There is a peculiar glow on her face and she seems to have changed into a new self, more alive and animated than earlier. After a while a young girl timidly approaches her and asks, 'Grandmother, what are you talking about? Whose last song?'

The old storyteller whips around and surveys the group as though seeing them for the first time. She then heaves a deep sigh and with infinite sadness in her voice spreads her arms wide and whispers, 'You have not heard about that song? You do not know about Apenyo? Then come and listen carefully...'

Thus on a cold December night in a remote village, an old storyteller gathers the young of the land around the leaping flames of a hearth and squats on the bare earth among them to pass on the story of that Black Sunday when a young and beautiful singer sang her last song even as one more Naga village began weeping for her ravaged and ruined children.

The Curfew Man

The night curfew was still on because these were troubled times for all in the land. Everything had been plunged into a state of hostility between two warring armies; the one overground labelling the other as rebels fighting against the state and the other, operating from their underground hide-outs and calling the Indian army illegal occupiers of sovereign Naga territories. Caught between the two, it was the innocent villagers and those living in small townships who had to bear the brunt of the many restrictions imposed on their lives. Of these, the night curfew was the worst for people living in towns because soon after dark all social activities ceased, even church services or social gatherings had to be concluded before the curfew hour began. There were stories about how people carrying the sick to hospital or in search of doctors were stopped and subjected to humiliating searches causing unnecessary, and sometimes even fatal, delays. Often these helpless people were sent back with abuses and threats completely disregarding the urgent need of the poor patients. There were several incidents where civilians were shot dead by the patrol parties after curfew and their deaths reported as those of underground rebels killed in 'encounters' with the army.

While all normal activities came to a halt after the curfew hour, for some individuals their real work began only after dark. These were the informers employed by the civil authorities and the security forces who were paid to gather information about those whose sons or relatives had joined the underground. They monitored the people who visited these houses; kept watch on where they went and also tried to find out what they told their neighbours and acquaintances. There was another group of people whose activities too, were constantly monitored. They were the sympathizers of the movement, many of them government servants, doctors, teachers and even ordinary housewives. It was this band of sympathizers who helped the underground organisation to procure supplies, medicines, and most important of all kept them well informed about troop movements. In order to detect and arrest the relatives of 'rebels' and their sympathizers, the government began to enlist recruits from the ranks of the bad elements in the towns and villages by paying them handsomely and sometimes even by threatening to reopen old criminal cases if they did not co-operate with them. These were the people who operated in the grey area between the government forces and the so-called 'freedom fighters', some by choice and others by compulsion.

There was, however, one among them who stumbled onto the job as it were, through a strange turn of events. His name was Satemba and he was formerly a constable in the Assam Police. Though he had not passed the matriculation examination, he was taken into the force because he was an excellent football player. His main job there, it seemed, was to play football for his battalion and he and his colleagues won many shields and trophies. But during a particularly rough final game between the Assam Police and the Assam Regiment for the coveted East Zone Trophy, he was injured badly. His knee cap was shattered, which meant that he would never be able to play competitive football again. Nor could he perform the usual duties of a constable because of this permanent physical handicap. He was also not qualified enough to hold a desk job. His disability became a real problem for his superiors who were trying to find a suitable place for him in the force. As they pondered over this dilemma, Satemba's wife, Jemtila, suggested that he take premature retirement from the service so that they could return to their village and take up farming. Though he had not put in the requisite number of years for regular pension benefits, the authorities decided to make an exception in his case on account of his consistent performance as a goal scoring player in the batallion's football team. So with a token pension of Rs 75 per month, he left Assam and went to his village in Nagaland to try his luck at farming.

Satemba and Jemtila accordingly embarked on a new phase of their life. He acquired a piece of ancestral farmland from his clan and began to clear it for cultivation. But being a latecomer and a junior member in the hierarchy, the piece of land that was given to him turned out to be unsuitable for any kind of sustainable farming. The dull village life and the hard grind soon became intolerable, especially for Satemba and so after two miserable years of farming, the couple came to Mokokchung town and took up residence in a small rented house on the outskirts of the town. The house rent was Rs 30 per month and so the two had to live on the rest of the pension money, which more often than not got delayed in transit. In order to earn some extra money, Satemba's wife decided to do odd jobs in people's houses. Such jobs were difficult to find because the families normally employed people from other tribes or even ex-labourers from tea gardens for such menial jobs. The few households she approached were at first reluctant to engage her, but she did not give up. After a few rejections she managed to land a job in a family with two young children where the mother was ill a lot of the time. Jemtila was an honest and hard-working woman and as word of this spread, her services were in great demand. Very soon she was able to quote her own rates and since she was a good worker people were happy to pay what she asked for. She worked in several houses each day and earned a tidy sum every month. But the itinerant nature of her work was not to her liking and she began to look for a more settled place of work. It so happened that at this juncture, a new Sub-Divisional Officer took over and as his wife was expecting their first baby, he was looking for a mature and hard working maidservant. When he heard about Jemtila and her work, he decided that she would be the ideal helper and companion for his wife. Jemtila was called to his office one day and after a brief interview was engaged to work in the household on a full-time basis for a monthly salary of Rs 100! Satemba was thrilled with the news and thought that if he too could find a job somewhere, their life would become more comfortable. They could move into bigger accommodation and maybe even plan to buy a small plot of land where they would eventually build a house of their own.

As the distance between the S.D.O.'s quarter in town and their house was considerable, Satemba would often come to escort his wife back home after work. It was on such a day that the S.D.O. saw him and began to talk to him, at first about general matters and then quite abruptly began to tell him that he was looking for someone to gather information about certain people in town as he had just come and did not know much about them. Would Satemba be interested? Satemba was no fool and had lived long enough in the town and seen and heard about disturbing things as a result of the turmoil in the land. He had also noticed how tense and suspicious people had become. Therefore he understood that the S.D.O.'s offer was not as innocent as he was trying to make it out to be. He was non-committal at first. He simply answered that everything depended on the nature of information the sahib required and whether he, with his physical handicap, would be able to gather it for him. The S.D.O. did not say anything further and after Jemtila's work was done for the day, she and Satemba hurried back so as to reach home before the night curfew began. After a few days, the officer sent word through his wife for Satemba to meet him in the evening. They had a long discussion and at the end of it Satemba was recruited as a government informer. It was certainly not the kind of job that he had ever imagined doing, but he was compelled to take it because he was discreetly reminded that his wife's job was somehow connected with the offer. Also, it was the first offer of a job that he had got after coming to the town and he was already beginning to feel uneasy about the fact that it was Jemtila who was the earning member of the family. In spite of his initial reservations, Satemba accepted the offer, setting aside his qualms in order to salvage some of his male pride. And so began the shady career of Satemba who would henceforth live in the unpredictable area between trust and betrayal and would never know the difference between friend and foe. In due course he was quietly introduced to the officers in the army intelligence network and more often than not, was instructed to deliver all important messages to them directly.

In the beginning Jemtila was unaware of the nature of her husband's work. She assumed that Satemba was to run small errands for the S.D.O., for which he would be paid a regular salary. It was only when he began to stay out at night, sometimes returning only in the early hours of the morning that she became suspicious and began to ply him with questions. Satemba admitted to her that some nights he did not come home because he got delayed while gathering some vital information for the sahib, which he could do only at night. 'What information?' she persisted, 'and those people you meet, don't they sleep?' He wouldn't tell her at first, but when she threatened to go to the sahib and ask him instead, Satemba had to tell her everything. Jemtila was furious, why hadn't he told her earlier? They could have thought of some excuse to decline the offer. She even suggested that they go back to their village, rather than have Satemba do such a 'hanky-panky' job, as she put it. She also threatened him by saying, 'Just wait and see, one of these days the other guys will come for you.' It was only then that Satemba told her how the sahib made it clear that her continuing in his household depended on his accepting the job. And he added, if she lost her job because of him, they would not only lose a means of livelihood, but also become suspect in the eyes of the government and anything might happen to them in these uncertain times. She still persisted, why didn't he say that his bad knee would not permit him to walk long distances and climb steps? And, she triumphantly asked, what about the curfew? How did he manage to evade the patrols? Satemba did not say anything and Jemtila quietly repeated, 'Just wait and see, one day they will get you.' This woman was by no means ignorant of what was happening all around them and how circumstances were forcing innocent, peace-loving people to turn to means that they would not ordinarily employ, just to stay safe and alive. She had to admit that they were indeed caught in a vice-like situation and every time Satemba went out at night, she kept a lone vigil in the darkness of their small hut and worried until he appeared at the door.

On this particular night too Satemba had come out of his house carrying information to the Brigade Major (Intelligence) who stayed in a small back room of the Army Headquarters in the centre of the town. Curfew was no problem for him because he was given the password each night by his masters to enable him to move about freely gathering or giving information. Tonight however, he was moving slowly because of his knee problem, walking in measured steps in the shadows and hurriedly crossing the lighted areas under the few street lights. Work such as this had become routine for him but tonight there was an uneasy feeling in his mind. He had, earlier in the evening, almost decided not to venture out tonight. There was a nagging worry, but he could not understand why he was overcome by this unusual feeling. The information that he was able to gather seemed to be important and had to be passed on to his superiors immediately. His failure to do so would have serious consequences for his career and he also knew that he might be 'taken care of' by his masters any time if they thought that his work was slipping.

With all these misgivings in his mind, he continued walking. He was stopped a few times by the sentries with their loud cry of 'Halt'. Each time he would give the right password for the night and move on. It was a cold night and his bad knee was acting up again. The doctors had told him that there was nothing more they could do about his knee after they removed the shattered cap. They also warned him about the intermittent pain he would have to bear as long as he lived. Tonight the pain seemed to be accentuated by the unease in his mind. He had reached the town square and felt like sitting down to rest his bad knee. He chose a dark spot and squatted on the cold pavement and thought about the message he was carrying for his keepers. He had obtained reliable information that an important meeting of the underground leaders of the area was to take place in the town during the weekend. It was an ingenuous plan: the church was holding revival meetings and lots of people from other towns and nearby villages were expected to attend these, and taking advantage of this influx, the audacious rendezvous was scheduled to be held in the assistant pastor's residence, which was in a secluded area of the town. Residents of the few scattered houses had already been given notice to go away for the weekend. It was actually a relative of his wife's who came and told her about this order and realizing that something of great significance was about to take place, Satemba made the customary round of his own circle of informers and came up with this vital information. If he could carry this message tonight, and if the meeting did take place as scheduled, the army could indeed capture the area commanders and inflict a big blow to the underground organisation. And for the briefest of moments he wondered if his superiors would give him a special bonus for helping them to capture or kill the underground leaders. But even this prospect of monetary gain did nothing to allay his misgivings.

Never before in his new career as an informer had Satemba seriously questioned his own motives for doing what he was doing; he preferred not to think about the rightness or wrongness of the government's method of operation. For him it was only a job for doing which he was given a reasonable payment. For some time, he was able to suppress his earlier qualms about the nature of his work and was becoming an effective informer. He had even circumvented Jemtila's opposition. But lately he had become uneasy about his own activities, especially after a particular incident in which, acting on his tip-off, the army raided a house in a nearby village. While the underground agents who had taken shelter there managed to escape, the owner of the house was arrested and beaten up so badly that he later died of his injuries. For many nights after that Satemba stayed at home saying his knee was giving him too much trouble. But the real trouble was in his heart. For the first time in two and half years, he was beginning to question himself and his so-called 'job'. This latest information that he had obtained was the most important development after the unfortunate incident over which he had spent many uneasy days of soul searching. Earlier, he had spent an agonizing day alone at home, debating with himself whether to continue doing his assigned job or quit, citing health reasons. His wife had come home early that day saying that sahib was in a very agitated mood and had asked her to leave early.

Satemba became more unsettled by this piece of news and vowing to himself that this was going to be his last job, had ventured out, bad knee and all. After resting for a while in his dark corner, he stood up and started to climb the steps leading to the brigade headquarters. As he approached a flat area he saw a dark figure move out of the shadows. Thinking that it was another sentry about to challenge a potential curfew violator, Satemba raised his hand and was about to shout the password when he realized that it was not a sentry but a total stranger who was wearing a black shawl and had his face partially covered with a scarf. The stranger motioned to Satemba to come forward and when he was close enough, quickly pulled him into the circle of darkness. He gripped Satemba by the neck and hissed in his ear, 'Go back home curfew man, and if you value your life, never again carry tales.' So saying, the stranger quietly vanished into the night.

Satemba remained rooted to that dark space. He did not know what to do. Should he do as the stranger had just ordered? What if his movements of the evening and the encounter with the masked character had been monitored by 'other' secret eyes? If so, the brief encounter with the stranger would make it appear that he was about to double-cross his paymasters. He stood there transfixed, like a person who had strayed into a minefield and could not take another step either backwards or forwards, without endangering his life. He remained in that dark spot for the rest of the night and when the sky lightened, slowly and painfully he made his way back home holding on to his good knee which seemed to be bleeding. Some pariah dogs looked at

him briefly and he thought that they would start barking at him
any moment and rouse the neighbourhood. But as he passed by
them, he saw that they were shivering in the cold and trying to
snuggle up against each other to keep warm. The limping man
was just another stray creature they could ignore if he kept his
distance from their space. When the exhausted man reached
home, Jemtila had just lighted the fire. He sat down quietly near
the fire while she prepared a hot cup of tea for him. Only after
he had finished his tea, did she bring in a basin into which she
poured boiling water and some lumps of salt. She then cut off the
trouser-cloth from his newly-smashed good leg, and began to
wash the caked blood from his injured knee. She saw that it was
a peculiar wound, which could not be the result of a fall as he
claimed. Even though the trouser had been ripped at the knee,
there was no sign of any other tear. She understood the significance
of this but without saying anything or betraying her emotions,
she dressed the wound as best as she could and after helping him
to change into clean clothes, led him to the bed. Satemba meekly
gave in to the ministrations of his wife and crept into bed, to lie
there the whole day and contemplate his predicament, which
forebode a dismal future.

When she went to work that day, Jemtila felt unusually light-
hearted and free because now that both of Satemba's knees were
damaged, he would no longer be able to work for the S.D.O. If
the first bad knee had secured him his pension from the Assam
Police, the second injury truly secured his freedom from a
sinister bondage. As soon as she reached the house, she hurried
into his office and told the S.D.O. that her husband had had a
fall last night and now his good knee was also badly injured and
that it would take a very long time for the wound to heal. She
also added that he may not be able to move about at all without
crutches. She wanted to take the day off so that she could look
for a doctor who would come to the house to attend to the
injury. The officer was struck not so much by the implications
of Satemba's injury but by the animated tone in which the
woman conveyed the information about it. She seemed totally
unperturbed by her husband's injury. Instead, it appeared as

though she was actually happy that her husband had lost the use of the one good knee. She seemed unconcerned about the consequence of this injury to his work. If Satemba could not walk, he was of no practical use to the S.D.O. and would lose his job; surely she must realize that. The officer was really puzzled by Jemtila's attitude, and remarked to himself how people of a certain class thought and behaved. He observed her apparent 'unconcern' with contempt and even thought of sending her off for good but then he realized that it would be difficult to replace her with another efficient woman when his wife's confinement was imminent. So he merely grunted to indicate his permission, reminding her tersely to come on time the next day. Then almost as an afterthought he added, 'Tell your husband that his services will no longer be needed. And also say that his wounds will heal properly only if he nurses them quietly.'

Having rid himself of the feckless woman as he thought her to be, he turned his attention to the urgent task of finding a replacement for Satemba immediately. He did not say anything more and giving a nod of dismissal to Jemtila, went quietly into his study and began to dial a number. In that brief moment between the outer room and his study, Satemba and his injury were swiftly forgotten and even the odd behaviour of Satemba's wife became irrelevant. There seemed to be something wrong at the other end because he could not make contact immediately. The officer was becoming more agitated by the minute and kept on dialing non-stop. After several attempts when he did finally make contact with the impersonal voice at the other end of the wire, he almost barked his orders into the mouthpiece, his whole body jerking in nervous tension. The response of the disembodied voice at the other end of the cord must have been reassuring because as the S.D.O. listened, his body seemed to relax visibly.

A new curfew man would be in place by evening and the man with the two smashed knee-caps had already become history.

The Night

It was a night she would remember all the days of her life. It was the night before the day when the fate of the baby in her womb would be decided. As though it also sensed the turmoil in the mother's mind, the baby kicked around in the confines of its watery world most of the night, making the mother more agitated. She could hear the even breathing of her mother in the next room, but her father seemed restless. He had got up several times to pass water and walked noisily on the bamboo platform adjoining the back of the house. She heard him clearing his throat and blowing his nose. She wondered if he, too, was crying. But that's absurd, she thought, she had never seen her father cry, even when her elder sister had died. She marvelled at her mother who was sleeping so soundly as though tomorrow was going to be just another day when she would wake up before dawn, cook the daily meal, eat and go to the field to battle with the weeds, trying to coax the crops not to give up on a poor woman and her hungry family.

The pregnant girl, whose name was Imnala, knew what would happen in the meeting the next day, requisitioned by the wronged wife of the man whose child was kicking inside her body. She would be called names of the worst sort, they would point out that she already had a bastard daughter by a man who had even refused to give the child his name, thus telling the world that he was doubtful whether he was the one who fathered it. How it had hurt her when the news was brought to the family that the father of her newborn baby refused to send a name for the child, thus casting aspersions on the mother's character! He had come wooing her when she was the reigning beauty of the village. Among her many suitors he was the most ardent, overwhelming her with a deluge of expensive gifts and daily visits. He was courteous with her parents, who thought him immensely suitable for their daughter because he came from one of the major clans of the village and was a junior engineer to boot. Instead of their strict vigilance when other suitors had come calling, they encouraged the liaison, hoping for an early marriage.

But things began to change from the day he sent word that he had been called away on some important business and would return as soon as he could. Days went by with no word from him, then months. And then news trickled in to the village that Imnala's suitor had joined the Naga underground army and had gone to China for training. Not only that, it was also rumoured that he had taken a wife from the female recruits of the outfit and was living with her in the training camp. The family was devastated, especially Imnala as she knew for certain now that she was pregnant. She remembered how one day he had persuaded her to visit him at his parents' house in the village where he was staying alone as his parents were living in town at the time and had succeeded in breaking down her initial resistance with words of tender love and passionate advances. From that day onwards, till the day before his disappearance they had met every day and made love in that house. When Imnala expressed her fear of getting pregnant, he assured her that he was going to marry her very soon and what if their first child should come a month or two early; it would still be theirs, wouldn't it? Completely bowled over by the man's ardour and pledges of eternal love, she became his willing lover and on the pretext of going to a friend's house, she spent those heavenly hours with the man she loved and who, she thought, loved her in return.

Imnala was at that time studying in the eighth class in the high school in a town called Mokokchung and was spending her winter vacation at home in the village. She was a beautiful girl and was accomplished in all the arts that a girl of her age was expected to be. She was hard-working too, a fine weaver and a great housekeeper. Her mother was always happy and relaxed when she was at home during vacations as Imnala was a big help not only around the house but also in the rice fields. But this particular vacation was to change the fortune of the entire family.

Now the very thought of this man brought an ashen taste to her mouth. Her daughter was now four years old and she loved her dearly, but all through these years, she refused to even take the name of the man who not only betrayed her but also humiliated her in the worst manner by refusing to acknowledge the girl as his daughter. But the villagers, who knew what had been going on, said that God shows his own justice to man: the little girl was the spitting image of the renegade father! It was perhaps God's justice to a wronged girl then, but it was going to be a different story on this particular day when an aggrieved wife was going to bring in charges against her of breaking up a happy family by her promiscuous behaviour with her husband. On such occasions, village custom gave the aggrieved party a lot of leeway: to hurl abuses including physical assault, within a reasonable limit, and imposition of a fine in cash or kind. Most important of all, the fate of the unborn child would be determined on that day, depending on the admission or denial of parentage by the man involved. It would be decided there whether the other woman could claim any child support, or if the child was male, whether he would be entitled to any portion of the father's inheritance. Imnala wondered too, if the child were a girl, would she suffer the plight of her elder sister? If a boy, and if the father cast doubts on his parentage, would he have to live with the accursed title, 'child of the street'? In Ao society, for a boy to be thus branded was to become a non-person. He could not claim kinship with any clan and therefore would not be able to sit on any assembly of men when he grew up. If he wanted to marry, whom could he choose, since he was not able to claim membership in any clan? For all practical purposes such persons are effaced from the social network of existence. Imnala was thinking, how could she live on with two such children? What would it do to her ageing parents, especially to her father who was now one of the patriarchs of the clan and who had had a distinguished career as a *gaonbura* for many years?

It was precisely because of old Tekatoba's credentials that the young contractor from town, the father of the unborn child, sought him out and persuaded him to be his partner in the road construction work. This young man, whose name was Repalemba, generally called Alemba, belonged to that new breed of high school dropouts who mingled with young engineers and were given small contracts as part of the government's policy to keep such young boys from joining the underground outfits. Because of his hard work and honest execution of the earlier petty contracts, Alemba had been given this substantial contract for building the road leading to the village. A big contract meant big capital investment, which he did not have and which he knew he could never hope to raise on his own. He was the only son of a poor widow and even though he had an uncle in government service, he was only a head clerk in the D.C.'s office with five children to feed. Besides, his uncle had disapproved of his giving up school and scoffed at his ambition of becoming a government registered contractor. They had earlier had a serious falling out over this issue and Alemba would rather die than approach his uncle for help.

So when he came to the village looking for a partner and approached the gaonbura, the old man at first hesitated: what did he know about contract work, how would he deal with overseers and chase after the bills in the engineer's office in town? Young Alemba said, 'Don't worry uncle, you can leave all that to me, all that you need to do is to provide the earnest money for the work and some working capital so that the work can be started immediately.' The old man spoke to his wife about the proposal; when he had finished she merely spat into the hearth where they were sitting and said, 'Why do you worry me about things that I do not understand? All I can say is, when will you buy the timber for the new house, about which you have been bragging for the last ten years?' He persisted, 'Alemba said that I can double my investment within a year, then we can not only buy the timber but the CGI sheets as well.' The old woman got up and said, 'Leave me alone old man, I am tired and I am going to sleep. Do what you want.'

In the end, the old man provided the required security deposit or earnest money as they called it and also the initial working capital and the work started immediately as the young contractor had promised. Under the supervision of the enthusiastic contractor, work on the road progressed satisfactorily and he was allowed to submit the first running bill. True to his word, as soon as the bill was passed, he returned half the money that the old man had lent him, saying, 'Uncle, this is only half of your capital that I am returning to you now, from the second running bill you will get the rest of it. The final bill will be made after the work is complete. I am keeping all the expenditure accounts so that we can have an accurate assessment of the profit, which we will share on a 50-50 basis.' Old Tekatoba was impressed by the sincerity of the young contractor and replied, 'There will be no need to show me your accounts; I do not understand these things. I will happily accept whatever you give me as profit because I trust you.' After Alemba left, the old man chuckled to himself and said, 'I cannot wait to see the old woman's face when I bring home the timber and CGI sheets for the new house!'

On the business front, everything seemed to be going on smoothly. But something else was happening in the gaonbura's household. Every time Alemba came to the village to inspect the work of the labourers, he brought presents for Tekatoba's young daughter, he brought meat and vegetables for the house and stayed on chatting until the old woman had to offer him dinner. Sometimes he would drop in when the old couple went to the field and chat with Imnala, regaling her with stories of how the girls in town were carrying on with the young officers of the Indian army and adding that it was impossible to trust any man these days. They could either be working as spies for the army or the underground or may be even double-crossing both for a few bottles of rum and a sack of ration rice, which he said was inedible after he had eaten the fine quality of rice in her house. Imnala was flattered that he was giving her so much attention and buying presents for her. Tekatoba knew that he was married and had two young children and so he thought that whatever kindness he was showing to his daughter was purely out of natural pity for an unfortunate girl. But as time went on, Imnala caught herself looking forward to his visits and had to tell herself to be careful about being too friendly with him.

One day when Imnala was lying in bed with a headache and slight fever, Alemba came to the house. Her mother was drying paddy on the bamboo platform; after a while the old woman said, 'Since you are here Alemba, let me go to my friend's house who is also ill. She had sent word for me to visit her. I won't be long. So please keep an eye on Imnala till I come back'. This was just the opportunity that he was looking for. He said, 'Don't worry aunty, take your time, I have to wait for uncle anyway'. After the mother left the house, he peeped into the bedroom and asked Imnala if she would like a cup of tea. He knew that there was a pot of tea already on low fire as was the custom in every village household and all that he had to do was to pour some into a cup and carry it to her room. Imnala was not really thirsty, but in order not to offend him, she said, 'All right I would like half a cup'. When he entered the room with the tea, he saw that there was nowhere for him to sit except on the edge of the bed because the only chair in the room was piled high with blankets and sheets. He put the cup on a small table near the bed and as he sat down, he noticed that Imnala was disturbed by his presence and was about to say something. Before she could do so, he quickly asked her, 'How are you feeling? Shall I massage your head a little?' Imnala, startled by this hint of intimacy, said, 'No, no I am all right' and tried to sit up, but when she raised herself, she was overcome by dizziness and fell back on the bed. He jumped up and rushed towards her in alarm and instinctively put his hand on her body. A gesture made in momentary confusion was all that was needed to initiate the inevitable. The touch so innocently executed seemed to ignite hidden fires in both and in spite of her awareness that what was happening was not only wrong but also extremely dangerous for her, she gave in to a primeval urging. They made love for the first time on her sick bed. Afterwards, without saying anything, Alemba went out of the room shivering, as though with a fever. When the old woman returned from her visit, she found him dozing by the fire, and when she peeped into Imnala's room, she found her fast asleep as if the fever had already broken and left her body.

What started almost as an accident grew into an uncontrollable passion for both and in due course, the inevitable happened. Imnala became pregnant out of wedlock for the second time. The village was agog with the news and tongues began to wag: 'What can you expect from a girl like that? The old man's greed has landed him with a second bastard grandchild'. The wicked ones joked, 'She too is greedy, you know what I mean?' and they would burst out laughing at their own ribald wit.

After the news of her pregnancy became public, Alemba's visits to the house became rare and Imnala remained indoors most of the time. When her friends visited her, she tried to tell them that he had forced himself on her. But even while she was saying the words, she herself did not believe this, and years later she would confess to her best friend that it was like a hungry person being offered a feast and that, honestly, she could not resist the offering! And this night she recalled how the touch of a man after so many years seemed to release a hidden spring and how the sense of rejection by a man she had once loved so passionately was being wiped out by the touch of another who was equally persuasive in his ardour. It was as if her body had come alive again and was responding to a natural impulse. Even in the dead of the night when she was thinking of the day ahead, the memory of that touch made her shiver again with remembered sensations.

When Alemba came after a long absence, the old man only enquired when the work would be finished, as though he was anxious to cut off all connection with this young man who had brought this new misery on his family. Alemba was stricken with an acute sense of guilt and rejection at the abrupt words, and tried to explain. But the old man brushed him aside and said, 'What is done cannot be undone. I am only thinking about the child'. Alemba understood what the old man meant; it was his way of asking him not to put Imnala in the same position as the time when her little girl was born. The young contractor did not reply. All that he said before leaving was, 'Uncle, the final bill is being prepared and you will get your share of the profit very soon'.

'Profit,' the old man thought, 'what have I gained from my partnership with this man but shame? My family has once again become the object of ridicule. I have lost face not only among my clansmen but in the entire village. Even the old woman refuses to say anything to me. Her abuse would have doused the fire in my heart, but now her silence is burning me more. As for that no-good daughter of mine, she has the audacity to tell her mother that I am partly to blame for what has happened! She told her that I should have agreed to let her marry the widower when he asked for her hand; at least, she says she would not have to be in this position today. But how could I have allowed such a thing to happen to her? She is young, beautiful and deserves a better husband.' Suddenly he caught himself and sighed, 'A better husband? What man will think of taking my beautiful daughter as a wife now?'

The old woman on her way to the field a few days later, was confronted by a relative of Alemba's wife and told that a meeting of the village council had been requested by the wife to deal with Imnala's case. This was the first time she heard about it, though it came as no surprise because it was customary for the council to sit over such cases. That evening when she told her husband what she had been told about the meeting, he simply grunted and said nothing.

In the meantime, Imnala had a message from Alemba telling her not to worry about the child, that everything was going to be fine. She felt like tearing her hair out and shouting, 'What about me? Is everything going to be all right for me ever again?' Her whole life lay shattered now, her mother had not said a word to her since the discovery of her pregnancy while her father rarely went out now. He sat morosely on the bamboo platform all day. Her brother came one day, only to leave her smarting with shame and hurt at his abuse, her sisters, too, came to enquire how she was feeling, not once mentioning Alemba's name. Her young daughter became increasingly troublesome, crying and throwing tantrums at the slightest provocation. In short, life became a living hell for everyone in the family.

Then came the day when, as custom dictated, the maternal uncle of Alemba's wife came to see the old man with the information about the summons from the wife's family to attend the joint meeting to be held in the presence of village elders. Before he left, he told Imnala's father, 'Make sure that she is there with the customary escorts'. It was not as if Imnala's father was ignorant of custom, but by saying this, the uncle was merely complying with a social duty. On such occasions, custom decreed that only maternal uncles or cousins on her mother's side could escort a girl to the meeting.

On the night before this dreaded meeting, the old man told his wife, 'Tell that daughter of yours not to open her mouth too much. Or else she may be slapped with a much bigger fine than we can afford to pay.' The wife retorted, 'You tell her yourself. Isn't she your daughter too? And that rascal. Wasn't he your partner?' The old man was taken aback by the vehemence of her retort. This was the most direct accusation that his wife had hurled at him. He wanted to shout at her but he had no words with which to counter her accusation. He merely turned his back and pretended to go to sleep. But all sleep eluded him as he recalled the events of the past year and half. Did he purposely ignore the telltale signs when Alemba's visits sometimes seemed unnecessary? Why hadn't he told him not to bring so many gifts for the family? Should he have gone into the partnership at all? There could be no answers to these questions except the certainty of the shame and ridicule that awaited the family the next day.

On that fateful day, as usual, the old woman got up as soon as the first cockcrow could be heard in the distance and started to cook. She knew that the all-important meeting would be held only in the evening as was the custom and saw no reason why she should stay back home moping or picking up a quarrel with either her husband or the morose daughter. She might as well get away from the stifling atmosphere at home and put in some useful labour in the field. She ate the morning meal all by herself and prepared to go out. But before leaving, she went to her daughter's room and hissed at the supine form, 'Keep your mouth shut tonight girl if you don't want the sky to fall on you and the child in your stomach'. Imnala heard her mother but she kept quiet. The old woman went out and collected the usual things for the day, tobacco for her pipe, rice for the mid-day meal, a small dao and a hoe and, picking up her tattered shawl, she went out to join the other villagers heading for the fields. She kept up with the others and even exchanged a few pleasantries with some. Looking at her, no one could have guessed at the emotions churning in her heart making her breathless at times. Beyond the village boundaries, she deliberately slackened her pace and fell back. As she walked alone for a while, all the outward show of normality and nonchalance seemed to abandon her and she slumped down on a boulder by the wayside. The tears that she had willed to stay within, gushed out with such force that she almost choked and she felt that the immense heartache hidden from everyone so far, was clamouring to burst out from the confines of her bruised heart. She had no control over these forces now and sat there alone weeping, for quite some time. She wept for the daughter so helplessly caught in the web of youthful passion; she wept for her husband who had only wanted to build a good house for the family and, above all she wept for herself for being a mere spectator of the sorrow now engulfing them all, including the innocent unborn child. She even thought that she should have persuaded her husband to accept the marriage proposal of the widower for Imnala. Now she recalled what her mother used to say: 'Remember, in our society a woman must have the protection of a man even if he happens to be blind or lame. A woman alone will always be in danger.' At that time she had simply laughed but now the words came back to haunt her as she sat there weeping for her daughter. She got up quickly when she heard voices approaching, and composing herself, walked away quietly before the latecomers could catch up with her.

For Imnala, it was another dismal day. Her daughter had suddenly developed a fever and was crankier than usual. She noticed that her father merely pecked at his food, which he served himself. Normally it was she who would serve him and fuss over him if he did not eat properly. Today, everything had changed: her fate hung in the balance, she would have to face and bear the scorn and abuse of Alemba's wife and the censure of society whose balance of justice always tended to tilt against the woman. A married man was equally guilty, but today she would be the sole accused. Even then she was strangely calm. She discovered that she no longer dreaded the outcome of this meeting; some mysterious energy was working in her and she was determined to face her accusers with her head held high. 'Come what may,' she thought, 'I shall devote my life to bringing up these two children in the best way I can. I shall finish my high school, get a job and educate them. I shall spend every ounce of my energy so that they have a better life than mine'. These thoughts seemed to revitalize the woman who had only a few hours ago, grappled with fear and utter despair in the darkest night of her life.

Imbued with energy derived from this new vision of life, Imnala swept the house, cooked the mid-day meal and managed to soothe her daughter so that, as the day progressed, the fever came down and she was a happy child once again. Towards evening, Imnala took a long bath and wore her best clothes. The father was surprised to see the change in his daughter but pretended not to notice anything out of the ordinary. The mother came home in the evening to a clean and spruced up house but she too, said nothing. She merely washed up and took her usual seat by the fire to drink tea and smoke her pipe.

When the maternal uncle came, accompanied by a cousin, Imnala was ready. The mother gathered the grandchild to her and watched her daughter in silence. The father got up to greet the escorts and taking the uncle aside to the bamboo platform at the back, said to him, 'Whatever the council decides tonight will be something your niece has brought on herself. I ask nothing of you but that you will bring back my daughter's body to me when everything is over.' Behind these harsh and seemingly callous words lay the fervent but indirect appeal of the father, which actually meant, 'Please protect my daughter as best you can. See that they do not abuse her physically.' There were instances where under similar circumstances a girl's hair was chopped off and her clothes stripped off 'to shame her'. The uncle did not say anything and the old man stood there alone, long after the party left the house.

It was not known immediately what actually transpired in the meeting. They only said that Alemba behaved like a 'true man' and managed to keep his wife's party from being too belligerent and abusive. Apart from this, no one was willing to say anything more. Very early the next day, the villagers saw Alemba and his wife going off from the village to their old life in the town.

When Imnala was brought back home by her uncle, the father once again got up to greet the party. Only the uncle spoke to him briefly and the old man thanked his brother-in-law for having fulfilled his customary obligation and said 'You have restored my daughter to me whole and for this may her clan never forget your great service. You have upheld the honour of her mother's clan in a fine manner. May the bond between our two clans ever flourish.' With only a nod of his head in acknowledgment, the uncle silently walked out of the house accompanied by the cousin.

Left to themselves now, the family did not say anything to each other, bur unlike many previous nights, they sat down to eat their meal together, as though by mutual agreement. Though the meal was the usual fare, every one seemed to savour it as though it was a feast. Imnala even fussed over her father and coaxed him to eat more, knowing fully well that he was only pretending when he said that he was not hungry. There was no talk during the meal but each one of them seemed content in the knowledge that the dreaded storm had come and gone, leaving them only a little dishevelled in its wake. After a long time, all three of them, Imnala, her mother and father welcomed the hour of sleep because they knew that there would be no dreadful spectres to haunt them from now on.

It was as though a festering wound had finally ripened and erupted, letting all the pus and bad blood out of the system. The pain remained, but at least the threat of fatality had passed. The breath-choking, mind-numbing agony suffered by the whole family seemed to ease off, leaving only a dull ache where it had once throbbed so relentlessly. Nevertheless, even if the pain should eventually diminish and disappear, the scar left by the wound would always remain on them like a disfigurement.

Imnala's life would never be the same again; she would have to fend for herself and her two 'illegitimate' children as best as she could. She would have to bear the stigma of being an unwed mother all her life. She knew that her parents would never abandon her, but there was nothing she could do to wipe away their un-shed tears or answer their silent recriminations. The one consolation amidst the chaos of her life was that her unborn child had been given the right to call someone 'father' in a society where acknowledged paternity was crucial for a person born out of wedlock. In spite of this social 'insurance' for the child, Imnala was aware that there would be many difficulties for her and her children. But she was determined to take life one day at a time, and tonight, despite all her apprehensions about the future, she would sleep well because her unborn child had heard the father say, 'You are mine.'

The Pot Maker

Ever since she became old enough to accompany her mother to the fields and forests, she began to dream of becoming a pot maker like her mother and grandmother. Her mother tried to make her learn weaving, a skill highly valued as an asset in any girl but she only wanted to make pots, and lots of them of various sizes and shapes. On days when she managed to stay at home while her parents and other elders went to the fields, she sought out the women who were expert potters and asked to be taught the skill. They were at first amused by the little girl's insistence; they thought that she would soon outgrow her childish passion for the craft. They told her that it was back-breaking and often frustrating work, especially when a sudden shower ruined weeks of labour, and the pots drying in the sun were destroyed by the rain. Some batches might be completely ruined if the firing in the makeshift kiln was not done properly. Out of a hundred pots, they told her, only fifty or so would turn out well enough to fetch a good price. The rest would either have to be used at home for various purposes or given away. They asked her, had she not heard her mother or grandmother ever complain of these difficulties? She said yes, but she wanted to be a better pot maker than anyone in the village and when she made pots, she told them, she would sell every single one of them. The earthen pots made in this village were famous all over the region and people from far off villages, and even from other tribes, came to either buy or barter the pots with produce from their fields. The little girl had seen her mother exchange pots for chillies, dried fish, and a wooden stool and at one time even a dao for her father in exchange for the biggest pot that she had made.

The reason why the little girl did not disclose her fascination with pot making at home was a conversation between her parents one night that she had overheard. The mother was complaining to the father about their daughter's indifference to weaving. She said, 'I don't know what will happen to our daughter when she grows up, she seems so reluctant to learn the craft, she won't even pass the yarn bowl properly when I am at the loom. She will grow up to be a useless girl and no man will want to marry her.' The father kept quiet, while the mother went on in this vein for quite some time. Eventually, he answered, 'She can learn pottery from you or your mother can't she?' 'Never', the mother's voice rang out, 'I shall not teach her this craft which has brought no joy to me and only a pittance for my troubles. Do you know how far that wretched place is from the village? Sixteen kilometres and a sheer drop to the riverbank; still we have to climb down because it is only there that you get both the grey and red clay required for making pots. You do not know how difficult it is to dig the clay from the hillside because you have never come there to help me saying that no man can be seen meddling in anything to do with pot making. It is woman's work. I cannot even begin to tell you how your back aches from carrying the heavy load uphill all the way to the village, and then pounding the stubborn clay inside bamboo cylinders to soften it. You have not felt how your left hand goes numb from holding it inside the moist clay while the right one wielding the spatula screams in pain with every tap on the clay. Do you know how many times I've dropped the mould out of sheer exhaustion and have had to start all over again to make one single measly pot? It takes months to bring out a batch after so much labour. And the reward? A few rupees. But if she learns weaving, she can make much more money besides providing enough cloth for the family. No, I shall not condemn her to a fate such as mine.' When the husband reminded her that they too need pots for their own use, she countered, 'Do you know how many pots we can get in exchange for a single shawl? Five, if they are big and six, if small. How many pots do you think we need, only three or four, which will last us for at least a few years.' Anticipating another rejoinder from her husband, she quickly added, 'Yes, I do admit that even weaving demands a lot of hard labour; your back aches and your eyes get strained. But you need not climb any hill and be out of doors in all kinds of weather. Weaving is not messy like pot making and can be done indoors in all seasons. Also the time spent on weaving one shawl is much less and the return is handsome. So be warned, our daughter shall not learn this thankless craft from me during my lifetime. I shall not pass on this burden to her.'

So the little girl, whose name was Sentila, started going to these old women in another part of the village to watch them at work. To see how the clay was mixed with water and pounded, how careful they were when they pushed their left hand into a lump of the softened clay and how deftly they rotated the lump as they started giving shape to the rotating clay with a spatula held in the right hand. The regular tap, tap of the spatula on the clay was music to her ears as she watched in fascination the pot emerge out of a shapeless lump of clay right in front of her eyes. When the pot maker was satisfied with the shape, she would gently lower the newly made pot on to a spot in her work-place and pull her hand out of the narrow mouth of the pot carefully so as not to distort it because the clay was still soft. It would take time to become firm enough to retain its shape. After two or three days, again the pots would be given a final touch up in order to retain the required shape and to test the consistency of the still moist clay. Only then would the pots be taken out to dry in the sun. After that they would be loaded on to a kiln in a uniform pattern on a bed of hay and dried bamboo and covered with another layer of the same materials, and then the kiln would be fired. The required temperature had to be maintained throughout the firing process. Therefore one had to tend the fire carefully; over firing or under firing would ruin the entire batch.

As it happens in any small community where everyone knows everyone else, the little girl's obsession with pottery became known and soon the mother came to hear of her daughter's visits to these pot makers. She did not say anything to the girl at first; she decided to wait and see how serious the girl was about this. She pretended that she did not know where she went on the days that she was left in the village to look after her younger brother. When Sentila visited the old women, the baby, who was ten months old, would be strapped to her back with a cloth and she would labour up the steep hill to reach their work shed. She would carry some cooked rice in a leaf packet with her on these trips. When her baby brother became hungry, she would chew some of it and, once it was soft, she would feed it to the baby. Then she would sing a lullaby to put him to sleep while she watched the women work intently. One of the old women sang beautiful folk songs while working but when something went wrong, she would substitute the words of the songs to suit her anger and frustration, which made everyone laugh. Sentila enjoyed being there but by late afternoon she had to leave them. So she would gently pick up her brother from where he slept, and deftly swinging him on to her back, would walk home quickly so that when her mother reached home from the fields, she would be there.

Sentila's regular visits to the old pot makers' shed became a topic of village gossip. People started asking why she had to go to these other women to learn pot making when her own mother and grandmother were renowned pot makers themselves. Why was the mother, called Arenla, refusing to teach her daughter the skill, which was her birthright? If all pot makers followed suit, then there would be no expert potters to take their place and the village would lose its status as the only village whose pots were coveted by all. Didn't Arenla know that in the days of head-hunting, this village was spared many times because of their skilled pot makers? As days went by, the gossip became open debate and finally, one day, Sentila's father, whose name was Mesoba, was summoned by the village council and asked to explain what was happening in his household, why his daughter

was making these regular trips to the old pot makers' shed to learn
the craft and most important of all, why was Arenla refusing to
pass on the skill to her daughter. Mesoba was caught in a dangerous
situation; if he told them what his wife had said about pot making
and why she wanted their daughter to learn another craft like
weaving, they would find fault with her and an immediate fine
would be imposed on her for going against 'tradition'. On the
other hand, if he pretended to know nothing about his daughter's
clandestine activity, they would not believe him and he would be
ridiculed as an incompetent husband and father and not only
that, he too would be fined. He pondered over their query for a
while and replied in a humble tone, 'Uncles and elder brothers,
I admit that we have all along known about Sentila's visits to the
old ladies and why she loves going there. She told us that a
particular lady sings beautiful lullabies and gives her sweet potatoes
every time she sings with her. Her mother has never said that she
will not teach her pot making; it is only that we wanted her to
grow a little bigger and stronger after her illness before we took
her to Lithu (the riverbank) to dig the clay. In fact, I have ordered
a small digging dao for Sentila at the blacksmith's just yesterday.
So what has been circulated by idle mouths is not really true. You
will soon see that Sentila will start making the best pots in the
village.' What Mesoba blurted out to the elders was impromptu;
it was a desperate attempt to avert their ire. But luckily for him,
what he said did have a ring of truth; there indeed was a noted
folksinger among the old pot makers who sang while she worked
and who gave a sweet potato to the little girl one day. Sentila had
indeed fallen sick just recently and he had indeed placed an order
for a small dao meant, not for Sentila of course, but for his wife
to use in the kitchen garden. After listening to Mesoba's
explanation, the elders decided that there was no cause to take any
drastic action against him yet and so they let him go, cautioning
him to remind his wife that it was her duty to teach her daughter
the skill that was handed down from generation to generation for
the good of the entire village. They also told him that skills such
as pot making, which not only catered to the needs of the people

but also symbolised the tradition and history of the people did not 'belong' to any individual. And experts were obliged to pass on their skills not only to their own children but also to anyone who wished to learn. 'Think of the teaching that goes on in the *morungs*, the dormitories for young men which is our way of educating our youngsters in the requisite skills for survival. In the same way mothers are to educate their daughters in the skills meant for women. Your wife should be willing to pass on the gift to her daughter.' And ominously they added, 'Anyone refusing to do so will be considered an enemy of the village.'

That evening, Mesoba went home with a heavy heart because of the rude reminder of how things were with them in the tightly knit community of the village. His wife's arguments did make practical sense but he could not ignore the logic of the village council, which always put the collective good above individual interests. And if he wished to continue living peacefully in that community he, or rather Arenla, had to set her personal objections aside and do what was expected of her. They chatted late into the night and decided that from now on, Sentila would not be left in the village to baby-sit her brother but would accompany them to the fields.

In the following year, Sentila was taken by her mother to Lithu where the grey and red clay was available. She was taught how to dig the clay with her implement, how to load it on to her carrying basket and how to soak it in the trough in the workshed before stuffing it into the bamboo cylinder in the right proportion and how to pound it. She was a quick learner and she did not mind working hard to achieve the right consistency and colour in the clay to form a sort of malleable dough. But when she tried her hand at the actual shaping of the lump into a pot, she came up against a lot of difficulties. She could not hold the lump of dough on her thigh properly; her moistened hand kept slipping as she tried to plunge it inside to hold it firm before the spatula in the right hand could start tapping the dough into the shape of a pot. The first attempts were disastrous and Sentila cried her heart out at her incompetence. But she persisted and would not admit defeat. The mother simply sat in a corner and watched the girl try again and again to transform the clay into a pot. Even if Sentila was doing something wrong in the process, her mother kept her counsel. Sentila would send appealing looks towards her mother who remained unmoved. The whole process seemed to have become a contest where the mother's will seemed to thwart every attempt of the despairing daughter to create even the semblance of a pot out of the recalcitrant clay. While Sentila hung her head in shame and frustration, the mother would push her daughter from the low stool and take over the job, wielding the spatula expertly over the clay held firmly on her thigh and gloat when the lump was transformed into a beautiful pot. 'Do you think that you can ever make anything like this?' she would spitefully ask her distraught daughter. These sessions continued for almost a year but throughout this period, the daughter was made to feel so inadequate before not only the mother's expertise but also her open disdain, that she was unable to learn anything from her. It appeared to Sentila that her mother's antipathy to her learning the art was putting a jinx on every lump of clay that she touched. Instead of her dream pots, she could produce only misshapen parodies.

The next year Sentila attained puberty and was required, according to custom, to spend the nights in one of the girls' dormitories. This particular dormitory was supervised by a kind, middle-aged widow. Like everyone else in the village, she too had heard of the discord in Sentila's family concerning her attempts at pot making. Also, the latest situation between the mother and daughter had become public knowledge. The older woman took to this serious young girl immediately and resolved to help her in every possible way so that the girl could fulfill her dream of becoming a good pot maker. She began to look for an opportunity to be alone with Sentila so that they could talk freely. But, in a dormitory housing almost twenty girls every night, this was not easy to do. However, an opportunity soon presented itself. One evening it was announced that a renowned singer was coming with his choir to sing for the entire village in

the village common. Learning that the lead singer was a handsome
man with many other young men in his group, every girl from the
dormitory eagerly sought permission from 'Onula' or Aunty to go
and listen to them sing. Only Sentila said that she would stay back
because she was not feeling well. Actually she had been looking
for an opportunity to practice her art alone and had smuggled
some clay from her mother's work shed for this purpose. It was as
if heaven had manipulated events to allow these two women to
come together for a pre-ordained purpose.

After all the girls had left, Sentila quietly took out the clay and
the implements from her basket and sat down in a darkened
corner to try once again to make a pot. At first she wielded the
spatula tentatively, for fear of waking 'Onula' who she thought
was asleep in her room at the rear of the dormitory. On the
contrary, the older woman was watching the young girl's clumsy
efforts with sympathy. She decided to wait for some time before
intervening. She noticed that Sentila was too tense, the left hand
held inside the damp clay was too stiff and her right hand was not
moving fast enough with the spatula on the outside of the lump.
As a result, the rhythm between the two was all wrong and the
clay seemed unable or unwilling to yield the right shape. When
Sentila wearily let the misshapen lump fall flat on the ground, the
older woman came out of her room and gently asked the frightened
girl what she was doing with the clay. She said nothing but
bending her head she began to cry silently. Onula went to her, and
putting her arms around her said, 'Don't worry, little one, I shall
teach you how to make a perfect pot. Come, watch how I sit on
the stool, holding my thigh muscles taut and make sure to use
sacking to cover the thigh so that the lump does not slip. When
you dip your hand in water before slipping it into the clay, make
sure it is not too wet. Hold the spatula toward your body and tap
gently like this. But most important of all, make sure that the
tapping is in rhythm with your left hand rotating inside the clay.'
Sentila watched in amazement as Onula fashioned a beautiful pot
right in front of her eyes and asked her to try again. She took
another lump of clay and with a confidence she had never felt

before, she started the process all over again following the instructions she had just received from the sympathetic woman. As she rotated the lump in her left hand and began tapping on the clay as instructed, she felt exhilarated beyond words. She was creating a beautiful pot! When it was done, she sat there admiring her work. But she was soon jolted out of her euphoria when Onula said, 'The mouth of the pot is all wrong.' Sentila looked and saw that indeed where there should have been a gradual tapering of the mould to form a neck-like opening, her pot ended in a wide chasm. She looked at Onula in frustration who only smiled and said, 'Enough for the evening. The others will soon be back and we must not let anyone know what we have been doing here tonight. When you work with your mother next time, watch her carefully when she is shaping the mouth of the pot. You are a quick learner and you will do well, but do not bring this work here anymore. It is not from me that you should receive this knowledge. It is your mother who has to pass it on to you. Remember, the village has ruled.' Sentila looked at Onula in a puzzled way but without saying anything, collected her tools and the pot that she had made that night and hid them in her basket. The next morning, before anyone else was awake she hoisted the basket on to her head and started for home. But before reaching the house, she veered off into the path leading to the village well and hid her pot in a clump of bushes growing nearby.

During the next pot making session, she observed how her mother held the left hand and the spatula, how she slackened the rhythm when fashioning the mouth of the pots and how a strip of elongated dough was added to the mouth to make the rim. She also noticed that her mother was giving her quizzical looks when she caught her paying so much attention to detail. Then, on a bright sunny day, the mother told Sentila that they should try to make as many pots as they could, otherwise they would not have enough days of sunshine to dry them. So they went to the shed quite early and began the process. As usual, the mother completed a batch quickly and asked Sentila to take over. Complaining that she had a headache and that her back was hurting, she went out to the shed after telling the daughter to try and make as many pots as she could. Sentila was surprised at her mother's assumption that she could make any decent pot at all and found it odd that her mother did not stay back to gloat over yet another debacle. With these confused feelings, she reluctantly slid on to the wooden stool and taking a lump of the clay dough, positioned it firmly on her sack-covered thigh. She dipped her left hand in water and carefully inserted it into the clay. Thus positioned, she took hold of the spatula and lifted it to start beating the dough to give it the required shape. As she lifted the implement for the first tap, she felt as if another pair of hands took over and was directing her movements. As though in a trance, she began to beat the dough in perfect co-ordination with her rotating left hand. The clay seemed to transform itself into another shape and before long she realized that the pot was ready. She sat there transfixed at her own creation, wondering at the dexterity with which her hands had moved as if in unison with her quickening heartbeat. The moment was almost epiphanic. She, Sentila who had suffered so much humiliation in her mother's presence for failing to master a simple craft, had now created a miracle. After a while she gently lowered the pot and started giving the finishing touches to the neck. When it was completed, she set it aside, separate from the ones her mother had made. She started on the next one, and like a sprinter who had suddenly found his momentum, she continued making pot after pot with the same speed and dexterity that she had noticed in her mother's hands. Finally, when she looked at her row of pots, she saw that she had made just one short of her mother's tally.

She realized that it was almost mid-day, and being exhausted from the labour she continued to sit on the stool and wait for her mother's return. She sat there for a long time, past the hour of the mid-day meal. She was beginning to feel very hungry, so she decided to go into the house and ask her mother to eat with her so that she would get an opportunity to tell her about what had happened earlier in the day. But when she reached the threshold of the outer room where, as in every house, the firewood was stacked and where rice was husked and where the chickens slept at night, a terrible scene awaited her. She found her mother slumped over the low barrier separating this room from the main one as if she was still trying to cross over. Her mother's *supeti* (lungi) had come unstuck in the fall and a white thigh was visible even from the street door. Sentila quickly ran forward and carefully retied the supeti to hide her mother's nakedness; only after that she bent low near her mother's mouth to see whether she was breathing. She was not. Instead there was a dried streak where the saliva had dripped. Her mouth was agape as if she was trying to call out. Straightening up, Sentila ran towards the village common where she knew that the day's sentries would be seated around a fire smoking and drinking black tea. When they heard her news, they all raced to the house, carried the inert body inside and laid it on the pallet beside the fireplace. One of the sentries was hurriedly dispatched to carry the news to Mesoba and to summon all the relatives from their fields. Sentila crouched in a corner, dry-eyed and speechless. Throughout the wake that night she was seated by her mother's body, muttering to herself. She stayed like that all night, refusing food or drink and not going out even once to obey nature's call. When the body was being carried out of the house the next morning, she ran after it shouting, 'Mother, I did not wish it to happen this way; it simply came to me. Please forgive me.' Those who heard her speak, did not understand what she meant, they simply thought that she was so distraught with grief that she did not know what she was saying. But there was one among the mourners who understood: Onula. Though she did not know exactly what had happened the day before, she intuitively sensed that something momentous had transformed both mother and daughter at life's appointed hour on that fateful day.

On her way back to her own house, she noticed that the door to the work shed was slightly ajar. Out of curiosity, she stepped inside and abruptly stopped in her tracks; two neat rows of newly-made pots stood side by side. Moving closer, she tried to distinguish one batch from the other to determine if it was the handiwork of just one or if a second pair of hands rotated the clay dough and swayed the spatula to create the two separate batches. She could find nothing to tell one batch from the other. She tried hard to reconstruct what might have happened; it could not be the mother's work alone because Sentila said that she went back to the house much before the mid-day hour, and it could not be Sentila's work alone because she was too young and inexperienced yet to accomplish so much even in two days. But if both mother and daughter were involved in turning out these pots, was it possible to differentiate between the two batches? Onula stood there for a long time as if trying to absorb a new phenomenon. When she came out of the shed, she had a dazed look on her face and seemed to falter in her gait. Slowly she walked away from this place of wonder, as she considered it to be, because she believed that she had just witnessed a profound revelation in the two batches of still moist pots, standing side by side in perfect symmetry inside the shed.

A new pot maker was born.

This story was first published in *Tribe, Culture, Art: Essays in Honour of Professor Sujata Miri*, Van Lalnghak and Siby K George (eds.), 2005, Guwahati: DVS Publishers.

Shadows

It was a sunny day. For the first time in six days, the sun's rays had penetrated the thick foliage of the jungle. Washed clean by the heavy rains, the leaves were shining like the newly-washed hair of maidens spread out in the open to dry. Steam rose from the grounds as the dampness of the soil slowly gave way to a new hardness and the boots of the marching column of soldiers no longer squelched. These twenty-one volunteers were chosen to travel through the jungle guided by a relay band of scouts who would escort them from territory to territory until they reached Burma. From there, a Kachin guide would take charge of their progress into China and then they would be in the hands of their Chinese handlers during the entirety of their training period. The mission of this particular group was to learn everything about guerrilla warfare and the use of sophisticated weaponry while they were in the designated training camp. The soldiers belonged to the underground Naga army. Though the group was marching in an orderly fashion, the surreptitious glances that were exchanged among the members indicated that they were gripped by something more than the understandable fear of the unseen enemy. Only one member seemed to remain untouched by this; his name was Imli and he was a last minute entrant into the group.

The selection of the recruits for such missions was done with meticulous care. Only those men who had displayed extraordinary courage in encounters with the Indian Army were considered. But this was not the only criterion; tribal representation had to be balanced so that when these men came back from training, they would be able to teach the different units located in their respective tribal areas. The planners were aware that all the members might not return, because regular army patrols were beginning to be deployed even in far-flung areas, and the earlier group, consisting of a large number, had suffered heavy casualties at the hands of these army patrols. This was a fairly new development; the government had recently become aware that the underground outfit was using the ancient trade routes between neighbouring countries in order to avoid the patrols. They were also able to ascertain that certain divisive elements in these countries were quietly extending their support to this rag-tag army. The underground outfit, too, realizing that their routes were now being patrolled regularly, had decided to reduce the number of each trainee group to a minimum of fifteen to twenty young people.

The small band of soldiers, therefore, was being extra careful in their movement through the difficult terrain towards their destination. It was a motley group drawn from the major tribes. Only Imli could be described as an exception; he was the son of the second-in-command of the underground army and his inclusion was seen as a serious departure from the norm. His presence was resented by the others not only because of the hint of nepotism but also because he was unaccustomed to the rigours of jungle life. He was born and brought up in a town and had no knowledge of the jungle as a village boy would have. He had been studying in Allahabad and had come home when he was told that his father had been inducted into the underground movement as a representative of his tribe. He had come back with the intention of staying at home for a while with his mother who had been ailing for a while now. But after a month of doing nothing, he began to feel restless. He felt that if he could not pursue his studies, he should be doing something more meaningful than simply sitting at home. So he sent word to his father, through the underground network, that he too wanted to join the Naga army. The father was furious at first; how could he abandon his mother to a nurse and a distant relative in her state? The son wrote back saying that he, the father, was himself guilty of that, wasn't he? But the father was adamant—he would never allow his son to join the underground army. A year passed during which the mother recovered enough to tell her son that he should go back to his studies. But Imli replied that he had left studies for good and that he wanted to follow his father into the jungle.

The distraught mother then sent word to the father to come and meet her, that there was a family emergency which she could not discuss through letters. Seeing that there was no avoiding the issue, the father arranged a meeting in their village instead of their town house as that was under constant surveillance. Imli spread the word that he was going to take his mother for a thorough check-up to the Mission Hospital in Jorhat, and left the town in a hired jeep. But, as planned, halfway through the journey they got into a government vehicle going in the opposite direction and reached their village in the middle of the night. As soon as they met, father and son immediately got into a heated debate over Imli's decision to join the underground army. Neither would give way until, at last, the mother intervened and said that her son was an adult and that he should be allowed to make up his mind about his own future. The secret meeting lasted till morning when the father left with a terse remark to his wife, 'One day you will regret this.' Imli and his mother then proceeded to their original destination and came home after a week. The doctors had found nothing seriously wrong with her, and only advised her to take plenty of rest and not to worry too much.

How Imli made his way to his father's headquarters remains a mystery to this day because his father had refused to give him any assistance in his 'mad pursuit', as he termed the son's obstinate determination to join the 'freedom fighters'. Imli's arrival at the camp coincided with the selection process for recruiting the trainees to be sent to China and with a mistaken sense of deference to the top brass, the selectors added his name to the list. The father's protestations were summarily set aside as

mere show of formality and ignoring even the reservations expressed
by Hoito, the unit commander, Imli's name was included in the
final list. The others in the group, however, did not know anything
about these happenings and considered him a liability as he was
so clumsy in the jungle. On a few occasions he would have
exposed the entire team to grievous danger had it not been for the
timely intervention of a member called Roko who had taken to
Imli immediately and made sure that he stayed with him all the
time, day and night. It was Roko who massaged Imli's legs when
they had a longer period of rest during the march; again it was
Roko who brought food to Imli when he felt too tired to get up.
Sometimes he even carried Imli's rucksack when he thought that
the leader was not looking. After marching for several days, the
group left Naga territory and entered Burma on a hot sultry day.

It was at this stage that they ran into trouble. The formerly
friendly Kachin rebels at the border refused to help them saying
that certain elements in the underground Naga outfit had
entered into a secret agreement with Rangoon to help them hunt
these rebels down in return for arms and ammunition for them
to fight the Indian army. It was an impossible situation for the
travellers: they were stranded in the middle of nowhere. To go
back without proper escorts would be suicidal since they had
narrowly avoided detection by patrolling parties on two separate
occasions on their way up to this point. And without the co-
operation of the border guides they could not proceed further.
Hoito, the leader of the group, requested the Kachin leader to
consider their plight and pleaded with him to help them one last
time. But the other replied that since he was acting under
instructions from his bosses he could not do anything. He had
been commanded to prevent their entry into Burmese territory.
Hoito, being a soldier himself, understood what his counterpart
was saying and in order to buy some time during which he could
think of a way out of the impasse, he asked the leader of the
border guides to allow them to camp nearby for a few days so
that he could send an urgent message to his bosses for further

instructions. The request, which seemed reasonable, was granted and the Naga group cleared a patch of jungle near a stream and made temporary shelters out of tree branches and palm fronds.

On the first night in the shelter, Hoito took his second-in-command, Chilongse, aside and they had a long discussion about what to do next. The outcome of this private consultation between the two came in the form of an announcement during the morning meal the next day. Hoito stood up and explained to the rest of the group that because of certain developments taking place on the ground about which the High Command may not have been aware, they were caught in this situation. Therefore, in order to seek clarification and further instructions, he was sending two members of the team back to headquarters, Roko and Lovishe, because of their experience in scouting and doing reconnaissance jobs in the past. He hoped that they would be able to do the job assigned to them without coming to any harm. They were to start immediately after the meal and were ordered to march day and night, if need be, and report within four days. Everyone knew that it was a tall order, but being soldiers the two did not demur and as soon as the meal was finished, they started with the barest of rations and their weapons. Before leaving, Roko went and shook hands with Imli, whispering in his ear, 'Be careful'.

After the departure of the two, the remnants of the fire over which their simple meal was cooked, were extinguished. They took care to use earth instead of water to douse the flames as pouring water raises steam and a distinct smell, which might give away their hiding place to passing patrols. Then each soldier took out his weapon in order to clean and grease it as this could not be done while they were on the march. Some cautiously ventured to the stream to have a long-needed bath. Hoito was a strange man and a hard taskmaster. He was also known for his unpredictable and violent nature. Confronted with this present dilemma, he became more taciturn and kept to himself, occasionally dozing off with his arm around his gun. He slept fitfully till late afternoon and woke up with a start. He had had the strangest of dreams. He'd dreamt that his father, who was dead for about six years now, had come to visit him in his house in the village and was scolding him for allowing a stranger to eat from his plate. He remembered that his father had a plate with a three-pronged stand made out of a single piece of wood, which he would not allow anyone, even his wife to use. But on certain occasions, when he was slightly drunk, he would call Hoito to come and share his food from the plate. He remembered that those were the happiest days of his childhood. Was this dream an omen, a warning? Was his father trying to tell him that there was a 'stranger' in his own little group? Who could that be?

In this mood, he went over the events of the past few days and was suddenly struck by the fact that there was indeed a 'stranger' in his group. Imli, the man who was inducted into the group merely because he was the son of the second highest boss in the headquarters and who happened to arrive at the precise moment when the names were being finalised. He began to feel uneasy about the way this person was recruited for the training. Unlike the others, he did not have to pass any tests or even meet the group commander, i.e. himself. He thought that everything about Imli's presence in the group smacked of the underhand and he began to get angry. He had always entertained a secret grudge against Imli's father because he had once reprimanded him in public for failing to carry out an order in the proper manner. This resentment was now extended to the son who, in his estimate, had not 'earned' the right to be in this elite group and was instead, becoming a liability. He was, however, somewhat pleased that the only person who seemed to be close to Imli had now gone from the scene. He had begun to notice how solicitous Roko was about Imli's welfare during the march. He had even seen him carrying Imli's pack once or twice. But, because he himself was fond of Roko, he had deferred taking any action about this. He thought that Roko's absence now was in a way very convenient for him. The more he mulled over the matter, the more convinced he became that there was an evil aura about Imli and that he was, somehow, responsible for their present situation. But what galled him more was the fact that he could do nothing about it till Roko and Lovishe returned from their mission, if indeed they did at all.

On the second day of their forced retreat, they heard voices in the vicinity and, fearing discovery, they immediately collected their gear, removed all telltale signs of their brief stay in the area and moved further into the thick forest. Luckily, they came across a cave in the forest and took shelter inside it. It was damp and dark there but at least they were safe from the heavy rain and danger of encountering the border patrols, which seemed to be moving at regular intervals in the area. Hoito was particularly grateful for the rain, which would obliterate all signs of their presence in the temporary camp. But the problem of Imli continued to nag him, adding to the anxiety of waiting for Roko and Lovishe and the constant fear of being discovered by the Indian army. They stayed inside the cave for the next two days, munching uncooked rice and drinking cold rain water. They did not dare light a fire inside the cave lest the smoke disturb creatures like bats nesting there, and also attract the attention of the alert soldiers keeping vigil on these border areas.

But Hoito was constantly troubled by the presence of Imli in his group. It was as if the humiliation that he had felt when he was reprimanded by Imli's father in public came back to him renewed manifold through his own father's accusation about the 'stranger' in his dream. In this mood he began to think of getting rid of Imli before Roko and Lovishe came back from their mission. But he had to accomplish this without raising any suspicion in the minds of his soldiers. He knew that whatever he did had to appear to be in the interest of the group. He was also aware that out in the jungle the outcome of his plan meant only one thing: Imli's death. And if he had any qualms about it, he managed to dismiss them by saying to himself that as the leader of the group he had to ensure the safety of his soldiers even if it meant the destruction of one who was considered to be a liability. At the same time, he had to ensure that he would not be implicated in any way with the actual execution. By evening he had worked out a plan. He would point out that if Roko and Lovishe succeeded in getting back with some new instructions from headquarters, how would they locate their new hideout? Was it not possible that they might even think that they had been captured by the security forces? He, as the leader, had to ensure that they meet up with each other without any mishap and move swiftly to their next course of action. He would then announce that he would send Imli to the spot where they had camped earlier and ask him to wait there for Roko and Lovishe and guide them back to the cave. This would surely test Imli's skill in the jungle, a skill that Hoito was sure Imli did not possess. With this plan in his mind, he called the group for a formal meeting and after explaining his reasons for this course of action, informed them that he had decided to send Imli to meet the two returning team-mates and bring them to their present hideout. On hearing his announcement, the members of the group were stunned. Everyone knew how unfamiliar Imli was in the ways of jungle warfare and some senior ones even ventured to express the view that sending Imli out of the cave would be unwise as he was sure to be spotted and either be captured or killed. Moreover, his presence in the area would advertise the fact that there were others in the vicinity and they would be hunted down like dogs and killed. But Hoito was adamant; Imli had to go on this mission to prove that he deserved to be in this group. Otherwise, he declared that he could not be taken along with them because on two earlier occasions, he nearly gave away their position through his clumsiness in the jungle. Though the soldiers were greatly worried, they did not dare argue with him further and thus, Imli's fate was sealed.

Imli, on the other hand, was beginning to get excited by his brief experience in the jungle. Whatever romantic idealism had first made him decide upon a life in the underground army had soon evaporated and been replaced by a new awareness of the ground reality. The constant and ever-present danger in the hostile environment only bolstered his determination to become a better soldier so that he could feel vindicated before his father. The strenuous march up to this point had been an eye opener. His physical endurance was stretched to the limit and the two occasions when he nearly exposed the group to mortal danger were due to extreme fatigue and a momentary lapse of concentration. But now he was determined to teach himself the skills of survival in the jungle and prove to his father that he was wrong in opposing his entry to this kind of life. During the two days in the cave, he learnt how to dismantle and put together an automatic rifle, which was in the custody of his unit leader. He also learnt how to walk in the jungle without making a sound and how to communicate with his mates through gestures and low whistles, imitating the sound of birds. At first the other members of the group were dismissive of his attempts and said that he would never become like them, but when they saw how serious he was in his determination and also realising that he was the weak link in their defense, they began to take turns in sharing with him the knowledge that they had gained from their experience in the jungle. Although it was impossible to teach him everything in two days, they were gratified to note that Imli was a quick learner and did not mind the gruff insults hurled at him whenever he made a mistake or gave a wrong answer. All in all, everyone agreed that giving lessons to Imli relieved the monotony of the enforced idleness and the constant pangs of hunger. So when Hoito made the announcement, Imli took it in his stride and thought that he was being given an opportunity to prove his newly learnt skills.

In the meantime, Roko and Lovishe managed to reach headquarters after continuously marching for many days through the thick jungle and eluding several patrols along the way. The fact that there were just the two of them helped, because they made less noise and, keeping close to each other, they maneuvered their way through animal tracks, ravines and streams to avoid the soldiers who preferred the regular routes. When they explained to the commanders why they had to return for new instructions, there was anger and disbelief all round. Who told them this lie, they wanted to know? And above all, why hadn't Hoito sent any written message? Of course the two soldiers could not give any answers to these questions as they were only foot soldiers and were merely following the orders of their leader.

That night there was an emergency meeting of the High Command and the next morning, Roko and Lovishe were given the order to march back to Hoito with a written communique. They did not know what was in the sealed pouch but after a hurried meal, and some provisions sneaked to them by the cook, they started on the perilous return journey to locate their mates and deliver the order to Hoito.

Back in the cave, Imli was given last minute tips by his well-wishers, and as ordered, he crept out of the cave at dawn and slowly made his way, taking a route which he assumed would lead him towards their first stop in the jungle. In the darkness of the cave, he did not notice the absence of two members of the group who had left earlier on Hoito's instructions and were waiting in a deep gully for his approach. Imli was being extremely cautious and therefore his pace was slow. Once or twice he thought he heard some noise in the bush and each time he crouched low in the undergrowth to ascertain the source of the noise. But he could not see anything because of the early morning mist brought on by the evaporating moisture from the earth. So he plodded on, sometimes on all fours, afraid of being discovered by the enemy. But what he did not know was that it was his own team-mates who were stalking him in order to intercept him and carry out Hoito's instructions. After an hour or so of painful progress, he squatted in the hollow of a tree to rest for a minute or two. It was then that the intermittent noises which seemed to stalk him earlier, materialized beside him. At first he thought that the intruders were from the other army and that he would either be killed outright or taken prisoner. However, when he recognized his team-mates, the initial shock and fear were replaced by relief. But only for a brief moment, because the two immediately set to work; they overpowered him before he could react and put up any resistance. They pinned him to the ground and one of them swiftly put a gag in his mouth. They had come prepared with vines to secure him and hammering stakes in the ground, they tied him to the stakes, spread-eagled and face down. All the while they avoided eye contact with him and Imli could see that one of them was visibly distraught. Having secured him firmly to the earth in this grotesque manner, they gathered leaves and dead branches of trees to cover him completely. Though Imli was making frantic attempts to ask them why they were doing this to him, his efforts came out only as feeble grunts because of the gag in his mouth. Without uttering a sound, they went about their business and when the camouflage was complete, they meticulously obliterated all signs of their activities and quietly vanished into the thick shadows of the jungle.

Roko and Lovishe had taken much longer on the return journey than they anticipated. They were both exhausted from the almost non-stop march of the last few days, their meagre rations were finished and their water bottles too contained only a few drops. After marching for three days, Roko suggested that they rest for the night so that the next day they would be able to meet up with their mates. So before sunset, they began to scout for a safe place to spend the night. It was Lovishe who pointed to the sprawling roots of a tree at some distance and suggested to Roko that they head towards it. By the time they reached the spot, it was already dark and, having satisfied themselves that it was indeed safe there, they immediately fell asleep. When they woke up the next morning, their nostrils were assailed by a putrid stench in the vicinity, which they had not detected the previous evening because they had fallen asleep immediately. But now the heat of the new day had intensified the smell and they immediately became alarmed. Rising cautiously from their positions, they signaled to each other to go in opposite directions to discover the source of the foul smell. They were both experienced jungle fighters and knew that what they smelled was rotting flesh. But the big question in their minds was: was it animal or human?

Circling in from opposite directions, they could hear the distinct buzz of carrion flies and as they followed the sound, their steps led them to the spot where Imli had been left gagged, bound and staked to the ground. What they saw lying in front of their eyes turned their stomachs. Death must have come at an excruciatingly slow pace and he must have suffered terribly even as life was oozing out of his helpless body. Nature and the scavengers of the forest had done a neat job. What remained of him now was his bare skeleton over which the flies were weaving a riotous dance of steel blue wings accompanied by a buzz that was several decibels beyond human tolerance. The hair on his head and even his clothes were ripped off and the bloody and torn shreds lay strewn all over the place. They knew it was Imli only because of his wristwatch which was somehow still attached to his fleshless wrist. In places where some flesh had escaped the predators, maggots had taken over; they were crawling out of the crevices between the bones, including the two eyeless sockets. Even the gag from his mouth lay at a distance, torn to bits and where there was supposed to be his tongue, there was only a gaping hole where maggots roamed freely. Roko and Lovishe simply stared at each other in speechless shock and sorrow. They were no strangers to death, and violent death most of the time, but nothing matched the horror of this sight. They stood there mute until Roko collapsed, heaving with unuttered sobs. Lovishe quickly went to the grieving boy and reminded him that they had no time to grieve. There was something more urgent that had to be done: Imli must be given a decent burial. So, silently, they freed Imli from his bondage, gathered what remained of his body and clothes and buried him in a secluded spot away from that place of horror. Roko wanted to put a cross over the mound but Lovishe dissuaded him by saying that it would be unwise. In this way, the inexperienced college boy who had joined the freedom fighters against all odds found his final resting place in an unmarked grave in the shadows of a deep forest in an alien land. Before burying their comrade, Roko told Lovishe that he was going to keep the watch.

Though they were hard pressed for time, Roko and Lovishe decided to look for a stream and follow the Naga custom of taking a ritual bath after a death in the family. They were aware that they had not mourned for the stipulated number of days for their fallen comrade, but the ritual of taking the bath would all the same signify that the mortal remains of a Naga had been consigned to the earth recently.

This completed, they were confronted with a problem. How should they deal with their knowledge about Imli's death? Should they admit to having buried his remains? Should they ask Hoito about Imli? These were questions fraught with dangerous consequences. They were veterans of jungle warfare and were aware of the underlying currents of internal dissensions and rivalry even within their group. If their commander was somehow implicated in the horrible death of their comrade, and if they admitted to having disposed off the dead body, they were bound to be viewed with suspicion and even hostility. They knew what Hoito was capable of doing if he felt threatened in any way. They also recalled how antagonistic he had been towards Imli from the very beginning. So after a long discussion, Roko and Lovishe resolved that they would not say anything about finding Imli or burying him in the unmarked spot. They would simply cite extreme tiredness as the cause of the delay in reporting back from their special mission. They also took a vow that they would never talk about Imli's death to anybody, not even to their wives if they got leave to go home. The watch which Roko took from Imli's wrist would be returned to his father at an appropriate time, and Lovishe was warned not to ever mention this.

When they returned to the camp and Roko handed over the pouch from headquarters, Hoito behaved as if nothing was amiss, only frowned once or twice when he was reading the letter sent from headquarters. The evening passed off uneventfully. That night the two scouts, Roko and Lovishe, slept the sleep of the exhausted after many days of stressful trekking and the traumatic experience of finding the gruesome remains of Imli in such a sudden and unexpected manner. But they were trained soldiers and never let their guard down. Early the next morning, they were ordered to break camp and be ready to march after their meagre meal of rice and chillies. Hoito waited until all signs of their stay in the cave were completely obliterated. It was only when they were standing in single file, ready to march that he started to speak, 'You know that Imli was ordered to go on a special mission to wait for the return of Roko and Lovishe from headquarters and guide them to this camp. But till now he has not returned, though these two persons were able to locate us quite safely. It now appears that Imli got lost in the jungle and since they have not mentioned seeing any sign of him, I presume that we will not see him again. What happens to him now is no one's fault but his own. So be clear on this point, no one is to be blamed for his disappearance. And now I want to tell you that we are to abort this particular mission and make our way back to headquarters until we secure the complete co-operation of our old allies. And remember, if anyone of us is captured, we do not divulge any information at all. Now let us march. And remember, be on your guard at all times.'

So the column of tired fighters began to march, single file, with Roko as the advance scout and Hoito himself in the rear. It was an extremely agonizing march, there was hardly any food, their uniforms and boots were in tatters and several times they had to lie in wet trenches to escape being discovered by passing patrols. Their morale was at its lowest; their mission was a failure in many ways, they had lost a comrade and were now heading to an unknown future. Roko, especially, was haunted by the memory of the horrifying sight of Imli's dead body. Once or twice he stopped himself from crying out aloud at the inhuman treatment meted out to his friend. But he forged ahead, subsuming his personal anger and anguish with the present need to protect himself and his group and bent on reaching headquarters safely. This the group did after marching relentlessly for three days. Their entry into the camp was unobtrusive, as if it was a routine matter for soldiers to return to camp in this manner. For two days they were allowed to rest undisturbed and were given as much food as it was possible for the cook to spare.

On the third day, the group was called to the barracks of the Commander to receive fresh commands. As he surveyed the group, the Commander noticed the change in their demeanour and became puzzled. Till now no one had specifically told him of the disappearance of Imli, the son of his second-in-command, who was away at the moment. When Hoito was asked about this, he gave the version which he had given to his boys just before they started on their journey back to headquarters. The Commander listened to him in silence and ordered him to write a detailed report about the incident. He then told the assembled soldiers that due to this new development, he was deferring their new assignment and that they were to remain in camp until further orders.

The atmosphere in their particular section of the camp once again filled with tension. The boys stayed inside, some trying to read the available material, mostly gospel pamphlets and the odd Bible, while some strolled outside aimlessly, but Roko and Lovishe kept to themselves, not daring to say anything, even to each other. Hoito seemed to be the calmest of all, writing his report laboriously and even whistling a tune under his breath. His report was handed in on the second day and all seemed to be fine. But during the evening meal, it was observed that Hoito was not in his usual place. Nor was he in his tent. No one said anything, only Roko and Lovishe exchanged surreptitious glances. The night passed off uneventfully. At morning roll call, Hoito's absence was marked and the rest of the group were asked whether anyone had seen him. No one had. By noon it became obvious that he had deserted and the Commander was seen going into the tent of his second-in-command. It was only then that the boys realized he had returned.

This presented a big problem for Roko. What was he to do with the knowledge of Imli's death? Though he could not say anything definite about what had actually happened, he could certainly guess how Imli had died from what he and Lovishe had seen. And also, the fact that they had buried the sad remains of their unfortunate comrade. Then there was Imli's watch that he had extracted from the body and which he had kept hidden; it had to be handed over to the father. Only then could the 'missing' report that Hoito had written be challenged and a verdict of death through foul play declared. The enormity of Roko's secret dilemma was matched by that of the Commander. Burdened with the responsibility of running the outfit on a shoe-string budget and beset by forces far superior in manpower as well as firepower, he was now saddled with the case of a missing cadre and the desertion of a ranked officer. He took days to come to a decision.

First, he declared Hoito a deserter, and added that if he was caught alive he would be shot by a firing squad. Second, he constituted an enquiry committee to determine the circumstances which resulted in the disappearance of Imli in the jungle. The work of the committee started immediately. To begin with, every member of the group except Roko and Lovishe was questioned individually and each one stuck to the version given by Hoito: that Imli was assigned the job of waiting for Roko and Lovishe to return from their mission and to guide them to the cave in which the group had taken shelter. When they were eventually called, Roko and Lovishe had a hurried conversation before going in for the interrogation and promised each other that they would tell the truth about what they saw and how they buried Imli's remains. As it so happened, Roko was the last one to be called. He was in the interrogation tent for a long time and when he came out, he appeared to be a changed man. He never told anyone, not even Lovishe, exactly what had happened there. He only said that when Imli's father saw the watch, he broke down and wept like a child.

The two friends were in for a surprise the next morning: the report of the enquiry committee was short, and it simply reiterated the version given out by Hoito and declared that the cadre named Imli was missing in action. There was no mention of torture or murder or the involvement of anyone in the episode. Soon after this, the entire camp was shifted to another location for 'strategic' reasons and a general reshuffling of all the soldiers of the camp took place. Roko and Lovishe were sent to separate camps and they lost contact with each other until they both 'retired' from the underground outfit during the general 'amnesty' declared by the Government of India some years later. They returned to their respective villages to live like ordinary villagers.

In the meantime, many other groups of the underground army made their way to China for training and many lost their lives in encounters both with the patrols as well as in accidents like drowning while crossing flooded rivers or falling off slippery ravines. But no other underground soldier seemed to have suffered the fate of the unfortunate Imli. It was only many years later that word filtered out from some unknown sources about how Imli had been murdered by members of his own outfit at the behest of Hoito. The gory details of his horrifying death gradually became the stuff of underground legend which led to a great deal of mutual distrust among the freedom fighters and many factional clashes. In his old age, Roko often reflected on this particular incident of his underground existence and shed many a secret tear for his friend who was so cruelly murdered by his own comrades. He was often heard advising the youngsters of his village not to think of joining any army because, as he put it, 'When you have a gun in your hand, you cease to think like a normal human being.'

Lovishe, on the other hand was not much of a thinker. He simply took up farming as if he had never gone away and many younger people of his own village were not even aware that he was once in the underground army and that he had served under the command of the notorious leader, Hoito. And what about Hoito? No one could say where he went when he deserted the camp. He never went back to his village. It was as if the vast jungle simply swallowed him up. The man, who had once harboured secret dreams of becoming a Commander and earning glory in battle, was written off from the rolls of the army as if he had never existed. Subsequent groups of soldiers who were sent to China on similar missions reported hearing from the natives about a mad man who roamed the forest, often shouting 'imi, imi' as if he was looking for somebody or something. They could not say whether he was a Naga or a Kachin or a mainland Burmese, because his hair had grown long, become grey and matted, his flowing beard was almost white and his teeth were stained black from eating roots and berries from the jungle. They said that he certainly knew his way about in the jungle and hid himself whenever he thought someone was approaching. But they did not bother about him because, they said, he was of no consequence to anyone now. So the lone wanderer was left to himself, to survive in the shadows of the jungle from predators, man and beast alike, and eating whatever was thrown away by them.

One day, this crazy-looking man saw spirals of wispy smoke in the distance, and he believed that there would be food where the fire was. He had gone hungry the last two days, his only sustenance being wild leaves and stream water. He was becoming weak and light-headed, so throwing all caution aside, he made his way towards the wisps of smoke. As he approached the area, he could smell the sweet aroma of roasting meat. When he heard voices, he crouched on the ground and inched forward on all fours. But, unfortunately for him, he was spotted by the lone sentry posted by the group who pounced on him and dragged him to the circle of men eating and drinking by the fire. This was the group of jungle rogues who had been terrorizing innocent villagers on both sides of the international border, looting, extorting money and causing general mayhem whenever they got a chance. They were renegades from all the different rebel groups operating in the area and were familiar with the tactics of survival in the jungle, robbing innocent villagers of food and other necessary items at will and dodging the army patrols that regularly raided the villages to flush out rebels who might be hiding there. On this particular day, they had got hold of some liquor and meat and were having an uproarious party, drinking and eating chunks of meat from a pig that was being roasted over a roaring fire. By the time the mad man was brought into their presence, a few of them were quite drunk. As soon as they saw him, they swooped on him, some tore at his hair and beard and some began to strip him. They began to speculate about who he really was and how he would look without his beard and long hair. Taking up the cue, one of them promptly got a dao and started to shave off his head and beard, while some others pinned him to the ground. Many cuts were inflicted on the hapless man as he struggled to free himself from their grip. When the hairy camouflage was removed, his features became more recognizable and as they now stared at the transformed man, one of the renegades jumped up and shouted, 'Oho, high and mighty Hoito, did you know that we used to call you that behind your back? Look at you now, where is your whistle and whip, with which you terrorized the young recruits?' The speaker was a deserter from the Naga underground army who had suffered, at one time, severe punishment at Hoito's hands. This was the main reason why he had run away and joined this band of renegades, where he was known simply as Boy, because of his tender age when he had joined them. He pushed the naked man to the ground and began to kick him ferociously, spitting on him and calling him all the foul names he could think of. He was already very drunk and was becoming delirious with an insane rage against the man on the ground. The others, who were not aware of the link between the two men, were completely taken aback by the turn of events. They had initially started out with the idea of having a little fun with the mad man, but the scenario changed completely once his identity was established and Boy took over. So they withdrew into a circle, while he raved and ranted and continued kicking and abusing the fallen man. As suddenly as it had started, the kicking stopped. The uneasy group saw Boy go to their temporary tent and come out with lengths of rope. They began to shuffle around with growing apprehension, murmuring, and some trying to talk Boy out of his obvious intention. But he was beyond reason. He shrugged off their restraining hands and shouted, 'The man who smashed my balls and called my father a woman deserves to die at my hands.' By now the man was almost unconscious, but all the same he was dragged to a nearby tree with the assistance of two reluctant mates; his hands were tied behind his back and they hauled him up to a sturdy branch, from which he was hung by his ankles, so that, as Boy put it, Hoito would have plenty of time to repent before he died. The members of this gang were no strangers to violence and cruelty but the sight of this grisly performance was somehow proving to be too much even for them, and one by one, they picked up their guns, canteens and also the meat and slunk away into the jungle. When some of them looked back, they saw Boy executing a drunken caper around the swinging body, still cursing and taking an occasional swig from his bottle. The man dangling from the rope began to moan. Hearing this, Boy went into the jungle and collected some prickly leaves which he fashioned into a ball and forced the gag into the mouth of the battered man. Once again he did his mad gig round the inert body now swaying gently in the void between heaven and earth. But after a round or two, when he realized that he had been left behind by his mates, Boy went to the dying man and shouted in his ears, 'Pray all you want now, high and mighty Hoito, pray that you die soon.' With a last obscene gesture directed at the unseeing man dangling from the tree, Boy threw away his empty bottle and groped his drunken way into the dark shadows of the jungle.

An Old Man Remembers

An old man is sitting by the feeble embers of the hearth cradling his right leg. Today it is giving him a lot of trouble. The pain is excruciating. On days like this when the constant drizzle since the morning has intensified the biting cold of the winter day, he should have known better than to venture our and climb those steep steps leading to his friend's house. Bur what else could he have done? Early in the morning his next-door neighbour came to tell him that his friend Imlikokba had died in his sleep during the night and that the funeral would take place in the afternoon. At first light, the old man hobbled out and made his way towards his friend's house to have a last look at the face which had become so much a part of his own. They had shared so much: played together as children, attended the village school together and left it at the same time. They had slept in the same young men's *morung*, wooed girls from the same young women's dormitory and even got married within the same week! When he heard the news, he felt as if a vital core of his own being had been wrenched off. There was no way that he could have stayed away on this day when his friend was embarking on his last journey, bad leg or no bad leg.

He managed to reach the house and found it already crowded with relatives and neighbours. Preparations for the funeral were in full swing. The digging party had already left for the graveyard to choose a spot and prepare the burial site. When old man Sashi (his name was Imtisashi) entered, people stopped talking as though at the approach of an important person. They knew of the close bond that had existed between him and the deceased man. Some people were aware of another shared association but most were ignorant about the fact of their involvement in the underground movement. The young of the village especially, knew them only as two old eccentric buddies who sometimes quarreled loudly, calling each other names and refusing to speak to each other for many days. But soon, overcoming their differences, the two would be found in the village common huddled together like young children, laughing their guts out over some private joke. As Sashi came in, people made way for him and found him a seat near the coffin, which was made out of rough wood that Imlikokba had himself carried from his field.

Old man Sashi took his seat and the moment he sat down, his leg began to act up. The effort of climbing up the steps to the house and the exposure to the cold were beginning to stir the demons in his bad knee. Several times he almost cried out aloud as the pain shot through his body and seemed to lodge in his heart, making him gasp for breath. He suffered in silence for quite some time because he wanted to stay on till the body was taken out of the house for burial. But the relentless jabs of pain forced him to do otherwise. He decided to leave before the pain became so unbearable that he, too, would have to be carried to his house. He did not want such a spectacle to mar the solemnity of his friend's last hours on earth. So he stood up with some effort and facing his friend lying in the coffin, began to speak to him, 'So Imli, after all, you've decided to leave me and go ahead, ha. When we were young, I could outrun you any time, but today you have overtaken me. But no matter, such time is not of our choosing. Go in peace, my friend and do not look back. I, too, shall cross the water soon and join you. Until then, Kuknalim!' When he had started to speak, the people noticed that his voice sounded young and firm; gone was the trembling that was in his normal speech; even the usual lisp on account of some missing teeth seemed to have disappeared. They were amazed to see him stand straight, bad leg and all (every one knew he had a bad leg). After the speech, without a backward glance, old man Sashi went out of his friend's house for the last time.

The trip back home, though short, was sheer agony; each step renewing the pain, sword-sharp. But he refused all assistance offered by concerned neighbours and passers-by. Leaning heavily on his cane, he took one painful step after another and by the time he reached his doorstep, he almost fainted because of the intensity of the pain. He somehow managed to revive the embers in the hearth and soon had a roaring fire going. Carefully, he seated himself by it and rested for a while letting the heat warm his ice-cold body. Then, soaking an old rag in hot saline water, he began fomenting the aching leg, cursing it all the while, 'Why don't you just die on me ha, so that they can cut you off like they did to Toshi? Sure, he has to walk on crutches, but so what, at least he does not suffer from any pain like you are giving me now, does he?' The fomentation and the warmth inside the house was a relief. After the self-ministrations were over, he dragged himself to his wooden pallet by the hearth and dozed off into a fitful sleep in which he dreamt that he was falling off a cliff and calling out to his friend Imli to save him, but that Imli did not hear him at all. He woke up screaming his name and found that the fire in the hearth had almost died out and the house was plunged in the gathering darkness of twilight. He thought that he ought to try and revive the fire and cook something for dinner. But, instead, he just lay there on his bed in the gloom of the winter evening. As he was about to doze off again, he heard someone call out his name. He sat up with a jerk; the voice sounded so much like Imli's. 'No it cannot be,' he said to himself, 'Imli is dead and by now inside the earth.' He sat up in bed, lost in conflicting emotions. Slowly, he first lowered his bad leg to the ground and, hobbling painfully, he groped his way towards the hearth. Carefully stoking the dying embers he once again managed to have the fire going. But he knew that he could not reach the hurricane lamp which was kept on the bamboo shelf just now, so he sat by the fire holding 'his bad knee. Then, he heard another voice calling out to him timidly. He listened attentively. The young boy called out again, 'Grandfather, are you there?' He recognized the voice of his grandson, the one whose turn it was to sleep in his house that week and called out to him, 'Come in boy, and be careful, it is quite dark in here.' The young boy felt his way inside without any difficulty because he was always in and out of the house on errands like this. He had brought a hot meal for his grandfather. After setting the dishes on a bench, he lit the kerosene lamp and watched the old man eat his dinner. When the meal was finished, he washed the dishes and stoked the fire once again. Old man Sashi felt new strength in his old limbs and started to talk to his grandson, asking him how he was doing in school, who his best friend was, and if he had managed to roll some more mud pellets for his catapult. The boy replied to all his questions in a desultory manner, which made his grandfather wonder if he was troubled by something. So he asked the boy to sit near him and asked him in a kindly voice, 'What is bothering you, my boy?' At first the boy kept silent, but the old man persisted in his questioning. After a while, he awkwardly asked the grandfather, 'Grandfather, is it true that you and grandfather Imli killed many people when you were in the jungle?'

Old man Sashi was completely taken aback by the question. He never spoke about his jungle days; it was as though that phase of his life was consigned to a dark place in his heart and would be buried with him when his time came. But tonight, the question of a disturbed child stirred old spectres and left him speechless for a long time. When the boy sensed that he had touched a sore spot in his grandfather's life, he immediately became concerned and worried. He rose from his seat and said, 'Grandfather, it is getting late, I must go back home and finish some chores. Then I will come back and stay the night with you.' The old man looked at the boy and simply replied, 'Yes my boy, and come back soon.'

For old man Sashi, his grandson's question stirred up the many painful memories that he thought he had managed to put away. It was as though an ancient attic door had suddenly come unhinged and all the accumulated junk of a lifetime had come tumbling out of dusty storage spaces, threatening to engulf him. He did not know where he was going to begin. Imli had often told him that the young had a right to know about the people's history and that they should not grow up ignorant about the unspeakable atrocities that they, the older generation had witnessed. But every time old man Sashi had hushed him up by saying, 'What good will it do them?' It was only now that he was beginning to realize that Imli was right because now his grandson was hurling a question at him from the other side of history. Even in the midst of grappling with his confused thoughts, he paused to salute the memory of his friend, 'Good old sensible Imli, how right you were and how wrong I was in thinking that the bad things will go away if one does not talk about them.' For a whole generation of people like old man Sashi, Imli and all their friends and relatives, the prime of their youth was a seemingly endless cycle of beatings, rapes, burning of villages and grain-filled barns. The forced labour, the grouping of villages and running from one hideout to another in the deep jungles to escape the pursuing soldiers, turned young boys into men who survived to fight these forces, many losing their lives in the process and many becoming ruthless killers themselves. Survivors like Imli and himself, did they not owe it to their fallen friends to tell the world what it was like to be fifteen and sixteen in the turbulent fifties in these remote hills they called home? Did he have the right to keep youngsters like his own grandson in the dark about the price their parents and grandparents had paid for a piece of the earth they now called Nagaland? But where would he begin? Should he begin by saying, 'When I was young like you?' But had he ever been given a chance to be young like them?

He remembered when his bad leg became even worse in the jungle and his superiors gave him permission to 'surrender' to the authorities over ground. But he could not go to his village immediately, he had to serve out a prison term first because he was an underground 'rebel'. The jail sentence was, however, commuted on medical grounds and he came home after serving only three months. It was then that the nightmares started.

Though he was making a valiant effort to lead a normal life as a common village, he could not hide the inner turmoil from his wife who would often shake him awake when he groaned and moaned and sometimes even shrieked in his sleep. Many times he would wake up crying and screaming because of his bad dreams. It was at such times that his wife would plead, 'Talk to me Sashi, tell me what is tormenting you like this. It will lighten the burden in your mind and your nightmares will disappear.' But he would brush her aside saying, 'Woman, you do not know what you are asking me to do.' The only response that she gave to his curt dismissals would be a look of infinite pity and sadness. Now as he sat by the fire nursing his bad leg, he wished that he had not been so abrupt with her and also that she was with him today. But she was dead and gone these past eleven years and here he was, confronted by the same predicament. Only now this question from his grandson was not a plea; it was a challenge.

When the grandson, whose full name was Moalemba, came back to the house, old man Sashi simply told him to stoke the fire, reduce the wick of the lantern and go to sleep. 'What about you?' asked the young boy. The old man said he was not sleepy, as he had taken a nap in the afternoon and would like to warm his bad leg for some more time. Moa went to his cot beside his grandfather's bed and was soon asleep. Old man Sashi sat staring into the flames while his grandson slept the sleep of the innocent. After a while he turned to look at the face of the sleeping boy and began to think of himself at that age. And his thoughts took him back to those days when he and his friend Imli played truant and went fishing in the streams near the village. He remembered too, how they scouted the countryside trying to locate the right kind of clay with which to make the rounded pellets for their catapults. They would dig the gummy earth with their small daos, knead it soft by adding some water and roll it into small balls. They would then dry the pellets in the sun to the right hardness. He remembered the few times when they had left the balls in the sun too long, they simply crumpled when they tried to shoot them at birds and squirrels. Imli was the better of the two in this craft but Sashi was the expert marksman, so they made a very good team.

But their most fantastic adventure was the time when they were hiding from a group of women returning to the village after a day's work in the fields. That day, too, they had stayed away from school and were trying to dig up a small anthill that stood on the wayside. If the women saw them and reported their presence in the jungle, they would be in big trouble with their parents. As they sat cooped up in a small hole trying to keep still, Imli suddenly whispered in his ear, 'Look at the middle one'. Sashi tried to focus his gaze on the middle of the line of women slowly marching towards the village with loads of wild leafy vegetables and yams on their heads and nearly cried out. The one in the middle of the line was stark naked and her breasts bounced with every step she took and he could see a darkness around the pubic region. Her newly-washed skirt was spread over the loaded basket on her head, drying in the last rays of the sun. She was walking in the middle of the row to protect herself from any sudden exposure to passersby coming from either direction. The two young friends were so shocked and awed by the sight of that naked woman, that even after the women had gone past, they just stared at each other as if to seal a silent pact that what they had just seen was never to be talked about, not even between themselves. Years later when he told his wife about this experience saying how shocked he was by the sight, she started to laugh and said, 'What is so strange about it? We women do it all the time. When we bathe in the stream after a hard day's work, we sometimes have to wash our skirts too so that we are saved the embarrassment of entering the village in a soiled skirt, and the one who does it on a particular day is made to walk in the middle in order to protect her.' He understood what she meant then but the awe and wonder of that sight always remained with him.

Now, as he sat looking at his young grandson's sleeping face, his thoughts went back to the question posed to him earlier in the evening. How could he explain to his grandson that some things in his life just 'happened'? How could he explain why his

childhood had ended so abruptly? And why youngsters like Imli
and him would be running for their lives deep into the jungle in
winter, which was the time of plenty in the village after harvest?
It was the season of festivities, but they had to go hungry for days
in make-shift camps, always hungry, always cold; but most of all
terribly afraid of the marauding Indian army that had burnt their
granaries and villages and that was now pursuing them even in
their jungle hide-outs. He looked at the sleeping boy and wondered
if he, too, had been as innocent and trusting at that age. After
those tumultuous years, he always thought of himself as old, born
old, and now after the death of two of his closest friends, his wife
and Imli, he felt older than ever with the increasing awareness that
time was running out for him too. As the fire slowly died out, he
went to bed with a heavy heart. But he resolved that one day soon
he would tell his grandson how his generation had lost their
youth to the dream of nationhood and how that period of history
was written not only with the blood and tears of countless innocents
but also how youngsters like Imli and him were transformed into
what they became in the jungle.

That day came for old man Sashi sooner than he expected. As
a result of exposure to the cold on the day of Imli's funeral, he was
laid up with a terrible fever and was confined to his bed. Many
of his old cronies came to visit him and cheer him up. These old
men, several of whom were also in the underground, did not
know many of the dark secrets, which only he and Imli had
shared. Others from the village were already dead, either in the
jungle or after being captured and tortured. The visitors would
stay for some time and then, once again, leave him alone with his
grandson. The old man began to dread these times. He felt that
young Moa was some kind of inquisitor who was bent on ferreting
the truth out of the dying man. Old man Sashi would pretend to
be asleep, or send the boy out on useless errands. The grandson
on the other hand, served his grandfather solicitously, trying to
cheer him up in his own way by telling him about his school, his
teachers and friends. But no amount of good food, or care, or
visits from relatives and friends seemed to have any effect on the

old man. He slowly began to withdraw into himself like an animal seeking shelter from an impending storm or at the approach of predators.

On the fifth night after he was taken ill, old man Sashi had a strange dream in which he met his old friend Imli coming back from his field carrying a heavy load in a huge basket. When he went forward to help his friend, Imli simply turned his face away and, without a backward glance, left old man Sashi standing in the middle of the road. When he woke up with a jerk, he remembered the look of rejection on Imli's face so vividly that he actually began to sob loudly. Though he tried to control himself, he began to tremble with every sob, which eventually woke the boy sleeping near his bed. Young Moa immediately went to his grandfather and wordlessly, put his arms around the old man's emaciated shoulders. This gesture further aggravated old man Sashi's sorrow and he began to whimper loudly in his grandson's arms. When the sobs were finally done, he turned to his grandson and in a feeble voice asked him to stoke the fire and boil some water for tea. As Moa went about the task, they heard the distant crowing of a rooster but they both knew that it was only the first hour after midnight when cocks crow once and go back to sleep. Old man Sashi, after five days of lying prostrate on his hard bed, lowered his bad leg first and then the other, and sat down by the fire gratefully taking the cup of hot black tea offered by his grandson. He then began his story. When he first started to speak, his voice was almost inaudible, and the young boy had to move closer to his grandfather's side in order to make any sense of his words. But as the hot tea warmed him, old man Sashi began to speak in a louder voice. Young Moa sat down facing him to listen to the rush of memories, which the old man was no longer able to contain in his brain. It was like the massive gush of a waterfall, which now threatened to drown both storyteller and listener.

'Listen carefully, young one,' the grandfather said, 'because this is the first, and the last, time that I shall speak about these things. They have given me nothing but pain all these years and therefore I did not want anyone to know about them, especially you. But now I realise that my friend, your grandfather Imli, was right, I should tell you these stories because only then will young people like you understand what has wounded our souls. We, too, were young and carefree like you once, but all of a sudden our youth was snatched away from us, and instead of schoolbooks we were carrying guns and other weapons of destruction and living in the jungle like wild creatures. I still remember how everything changed for me and my friend, Imli. It was the last day of school in December before the Christmas holidays and all of us were excited, nobody paid any attention to what the teacher was saying. We were talking loudly to each other about our plans for the holidays. Imli and I had made plenty of pellets for our catapults and were looking forward to camping out in our farmhouses away from the village and shooting down the birds that come there in great flocks to eat the leftover grain after harvest. Of course, you know, that this is the time when the birds taste best and as we made our plans, our mouths watered at the prospect of eating their succulent meat. But it was not to be. Even as the last peal of the school bell was dying away, we heard a great roar, of women and children shrieking and crying and trying to run away from the balls of fire which seemed to be chasing them. All the school children rushed out and we saw the most horrifying sight of our lives. At that time of day, as you know, the only people left in the village are children, nursing mothers, old people who can no longer go to the fields and a few village sentries. It was these helpless ones that the gun-toting soldiers were picking out easily and shooting like animals running away from a forest fire. One village sentry was running towards the school, shouting at the top of his voice, "Run to the jungle, run to the jungle." We were paralysed with fear and shock and simply stood where we were. But he kept on running and shouting, his voice now gone hoarse from shouting and from the smoke he inhaled with every word. At last our teacher took up the cry and instructed us to scatter in different directions towards the jungle, telling us to go as far as we could go before nightfall. He added, "Stay together in small groups and do' not make a noise or light any fire wherever you may be. We will come for you in the morning. Now run, run for your lives." I quickly took hold of Imli's hand and began to pull him away from the school compound. But he did not turn or move towards the path I had chosen for us. Instead he was moaning and pointing to a figure just below us on the village path. It was the sentry and some soldiers wearing heavy boots and helmets were beating him up. I cried out to him, "Come on Imli, otherwise those soldiers will catch us too and kill us." Still he did not move and, instead, made as if he would go towards the fallen man. I held on to him tightly, not letting him go and craned my neck to see the man on the ground. His face was unrecognizable, a bloody mess, but because we were standing at a higher level, I could make out what he was wearing. It was only then that I realised why Imli was behaving in this manner: the inert man on the ground was his father who was on village sentry duty that day and was coming to warn the schoolchildren to run away from the village. As though my recognising his father was the cue he needed, Imli began to whimper like a hurt animal. It took all my strength to pull him away from the spot and drag him towards the jungle. By that time of course, all the other students, young and old, had disappeared into the jungle and we found ourselves separated from the main group.

By the time we reached the edge of the forest, away from the mayhem in the village, it was already dark. We were hungry, we were cold, but most of all we were terrified, not knowing where we were heading. The eerie jungle sounds were beginning to grow in volume, which only added to our fear. With great difficulty, we crawled our way in to a huge tree-trunk and holding each other tightly, we tried to rest for a while. But rest would not come because every now and then, Imli's body would go into terrible convulsions, with unearthly groans coming out of the depths of his being. He was remembering the sight of his father's battered body lying so helplessly in the dust of the ravaged village. It took all my strength and determination to keep him from becoming completely hysterical and breaking away from the hold of my weakening arms. Fortunately, the terrible physical and mental agony he had undergone exhausted him and he fell into a fitful sleep. After a while, I, too, finally began to doze off and fell into a deep sleep.

But we were in for a greater shock in the morning. When we woke up to the birdsong that surrounded us, still holding onto each other, the scene that confronted us seemed to be a picture out of hell. Half a dozen dirty, bearded and longhaired creatures were standing beside us pointing their guns at our heads. We thought that we were already dead. Our mouths fell open but no sound came out though we were trying to scream. Our bodies lay still and lifeless though we wanted get up and sprint to safety in the jungle. I do not know how long we stayed like that but only remember marching alongside these creatures deeper into the forest, stopping only once to eat some scraps of food they were carrying and drinking from a tiny waterfall hidden by tall ferns. Eventually we crossed a small river, which was almost dry and entering another forest, suddenly came upon a clearing dotted with small hutments. We could smell wood fire mingled with the aroma of rice and meat being cooked. All through the trek, someone who appeared to be the leader of the group stayed near us and even helped Imli several times when he stumbled and fell, without saying a word. But as we were about to enter the clearing, he drew us aside and spoke for the first time and wonder of wonders, in our own dialect! We were so stunned that we remained mute though we understood what he was saying. He was telling us that we were safe here but that we should not say a word about what had happened in the village the day before to anyone in the camp. When he said 'camp' we immediately realized that we were in the hands of underground soldiers.

We were led to a secluded section of the camp and told not stir out except when summoned. We were given food, some used clothes and told to bathe in the small stream adjacent to our hut. We did as we were told and returned to our allotted space among the strangers. We did not reveal that we belonged to the same village as the leader of the scouting party. That night we tried to sleep but the uncertainty about our future and anxiety about our loved ones kept us awake most of the night. Towards daybreak we must have fallen asleep because when we were shaken awake, the camp was already dismantled and the party about to march off to an unknown destination. We followed them meekly on empty stomachs because we did not know what their reaction might be if we dared to ask for food. The mid-day halt was short and the little food that we received merely made us hungrier. But the march went on relentlessly until the sun was about to set. Bringing the column to a halt, the leader sent a few scouts to look for a suitable site to set up camp for the night. When one was located deep in the jungle, we were herded into the makeshift lodging where we spent another miserable night bothered by jungle sounds and bitten by mosquitoes. The next morning was no better; after a scanty meal of cold rice and salt, we marched again. But it got worse as the topography of the land changed, and we found ourselves following steep animal trails to reach our destination. It took us nearly two hours to make our way to the hilltop beyond which our final destination seemed to be located. By early evening we reached it and what a surprise it turned out to be.

The training camp, was at the base of the steep hill we had climbed earlier and was surrounded by even higher hills in the other three directions. It was a veritable fortress in the valley with the hills providing natural protection. It was here that our jungle life began. We were told that we had been recruited into the Naga National Army and that we would be given proper training here. We had to take an oath to remain loyal and if at any time we attempted to run away or betray the others, we would be shot. We stayed there for nearly a year during which time we learnt to forget family, friends and everything to do with our former life. Soldiers we were made into and that's what we resolved to remain. Imli and I did not talk openly in front of the others who belonged to other villages. We had developed a cunning that we did not know we were capable of. But we shared a tacit understanding that we would look out for each other at all times and that we would bide our time until we found an opportunity to run away.

That was our dream; to escape and go back to our village and be reunited with our families. It was that dream that kept us going.

But it was soon to be shattered. In a pre-dawn raid the army attacked our camp and we were caught completely by surprise. The location of the camp was thought to be so secure that the commander had slackened the vigilance by posting just two sentries, who in turn became negligent. Now we were about to pay the price with our lives. Imli and I looked at each other asking the silent question: can we make a break for it? Almost imperceptibly we nodded and grabbing the rifles we had cleaned the night before, we crept towards the store to steal some bullets. There was chaos in this part of the camp, with everyone clamouring for bullets. We too joined the line to receive our share. The commander was shouting, 'Make every bullet count.' We took the bullets and scampered out as if to join the fight, but as soon as we cleared the perimeter, we sprinted away from the fighting and made for the thick jungle. We kept on marching until nightfall and spent a horrible night on the peak of the hill; hungry, cold, and desperately anxious to make our way to the village we were forced to flee from ten months ago. Sprinting downhill we stumbled on to a small spring where we drank the crystal clear water and continued on our way. At dusk on the third day we reached the outskirts of the village and stopped in our tracks: it was burnt to ashes and inhabited only by a lone scrawny limping piglet which had somehow escaped the general slaughter and was now scrounging in the decay and desolation of the abandoned village. Imli and I spent the night in the open at the same spot where our school used to stand.

Before daybreak, we marched out towards where the granaries once stood. Here, too, the same scenario greeted us. As we were desperately hungry, we began to rummage in the ruins of the granaries. At the far end of the row, we came upon a partially gutted one. What the fire could not complete, it seemed, the elements had pitched in to finish. The structure had fallen into itself and rotting bamboo posts and walls stood out incongruously in a grey heap among the blackened masses of the other sites.

Sensing that there might still be something salvageable under the heap, we frantically removed the debris and, wonder of wonders, we found an earthen pot, you know the kind where husked rice is stored? It was one of those, and although its mouth was broken, the rest of it seemed to be intact. Plunging a hand inside, we discovered that it had contained some special sticky rice, which was now almost powdery to our touch. No matter: we ate mouthfuls of that treasure; we were so hungry that we would perhaps have swallowed even the ashes around us. We carefully packed the rest of the powdery rice in leaf packages and decided to track down the other villagers who, we were sure, had found shelter in a jungle hideout. We had learnt to be stealthy in our movements, but it took us almost the whole day to scout the area. Towards evening we saw some faint traces of smoke rising to the sky in the west of our old village. It was a heavily wooded area and our people believed that it was where the spirits of the forest lived. We were not surprised that the villagers chose this place to hide because even if the hideout were discovered, no local guide would dare to lead any patrolling party to the forest because of this superstition.

Imli and I discussed how best we could alert the villagers of our presence; if we surprised them, taking us to be hostile, they might do us bodily harm before we had time to tell our story. So we waited until nightfall to reveal ourselves to them. It was Imli who came up with the brilliant idea of using birdcalls in the darkness. As children we had learnt different birdcalls to convey messages across the far-flung rice paddies. Hoping that at least some of our friends would be among the survivors, Imli let out a soft tentative whoop like an owl, followed by a twittering sound. No response. He tried again, still no return whoop or twitter. We almost gave up, not because we did not want to join the group but because we were faint with hunger and pain. 'I'll give it a last try,' Imli said and taking a deep breath let out another whoop. The strength and tone of that sound was so deep that I thought his lungs had burst because he collapsed even as the last note left his body. I slipped to his side to see if he was all right and tried to raise him from the ground where he lay in a heap. Seconds after I reached him, there was an answering whoop followed by a long twittering echo. I could not hold myself any longer and cried out loud, 'Here, we are here, both Imli and I.' We waited fearfully. After what seemed to be an eternity, we saw the faint light of reed-burning firesticks approaching our position. We also saw that it was a big group of armed men; the villagers were taking no chances. They recognized us and when they saw our condition, with Imli still lying on the ground, they made a makeshift stretcher and carried him to the shelter while I hobbled after them. We were taken directly to the headman's lodge, our weapons were stored away and after asking a few questions, he declared that we were to be washed and given fresh clothing and food and that we were to spend the night there under guard. We were so exhausted from our ordeal that even though we wanted to ask about our families, we simply collapsed on our mats and slept like the dead.

When we woke up the next morning, many of our relatives were waiting to meet us; they included my old mother, brothers and my only sister. Imli of course knew that he would not see his father, whom we both saw lying below our school in a bloody heap; yet when an old man drifted into view, he leapt out of the mat where we slept and ran towards him. It was indeed his father, but what a sight: his face was disfigured almost beyond recognition, he had a limp and one eye was missing. Imli stood there as though paralysed; it was the father who called out to him and he walked towards him in a daze. No words were exchanged, but to this day I can see the look of wonder and horror that my friend had on his face as he shook his father's hand. His mother and sister silently watched the painful reunion. Our joy at meeting up with our families was, however, short-lived. A few days later, scouts came with the unsettling news that a large convoy was heading towards the area where the displaced villagers were hiding and they said that we might be the target. We made preparations to flee from the present location deeper into the jungle. So, in the evening, we struck camp and we were once again on the move. Before leaving, Imli and I resolved that we would stay close to each other and use our weapons, which were given back to us, if necessary. We told the elders that since we were among the few who had guns, we two should be allowed to bring up the rear and put up a fight if the need arose. They agreed and with the help of the faint moonlight, the terrified villagers started out on yet another exodus in search of a safer home. We marched all night and when the eastern sky began to brighten, a short halt was announced so that we could eat the little food that we were able to bring along.

It was at this point that I had a great idea, what if Imli and I lay a trap for the army patrols that walk on foot along the road, after leaving the vehicles in which they travel a little way behind them? At first Imli was aghast and asked me if I had gone crazy. I said no, it just might work! It took me a long time to persuade Imli to agree to my plan. After that I approached the elders and told them of our plan. Predictably, they too were aghast at the audacity and, as one elder pointed out, the suicidal consequences of the enterprise. But I stuck to my suggestion, telling them that if we two were found in the group, things would be much worse for the entire village. We were recruits of the underground army and hence 'enemies'. If we were not with them, the worst that could happen to them would be some beatings and eventual incarceration in the 'grouping' zones. But if we were found there, who knows, the entire village might be wiped out. Even as I was saying this, I was wondering from where I had picked up these arguments. However, they seemed to be working. After a hurried consultation among themselves, they agreed and so we parted ways there. We slackened our pace and no longer followed the group marching deeper into the jungle to locate another hideout. The two of us went into the jungle and began to work on our plan. We collected vines from the forest and twined them into sturdy ropes. We cut down lengths of bamboo and after splitting them open, sharpened the edges to sword-points and wove these into small stockade-like structures. But our problem was we had no food; so we spent an entire day foraging and hunting with our daos in the jungle. We were lucky to came across an abandoned farmhouse where we discovered some mouldy rice, which we cooked in bamboo cylinders over an open fire. Imli

went fishing in a nearby stream and caught some shrimps, which
we cooked in the same manner. Being exhausted and hungry from
our long march, we decided to spend the night at the farmhouse.
As we were about to go to sleep, we heard a noise and peering into
the darkness outside, we detected some movement in the dim
light of a late-rising moon. Dark shapes were stealthily approaching
the farmhouse with what appeared to be to be drawn weapons.
There was no time to panic or run; we had to do something if we
were to save ourselves. Luckily, we had the sharpened bamboo
stakes with us and we began to create a structure to put up at the
door, which would pierce anyone who entered. We knew that the
spikes would merely form a stumbling block without causing any
real harm to the intruders. So, we hurriedly created two mounds
with anything that came handy, and laid them one on each side
of the fireplace to simulate two sleeping figures. We then retreated
to opposite corners of the small farmhouse, our guns at the ready.
We hoped that the fake figures would fool them for a while and
give us an opportunity to use our weapons. When we had last
looked out we had seen four or five men crawling uphill to "there
we were hiding. Their progress was slow as they were trying to
make as little noise as possible, and, I suspect, they too were
apprehensive about what they would encounter inside the
farmhouse. So they were being very cautious and taking their
time in launching their assault.

They took a long time approaching the farmhouse. We
strained our eyes in the dark to make out how many men were in
the group. There were five, of whom two were advance scouts.
These two entered the farmhouse cautiously. We had purposely
left the door ajar and after a cursory survey they signaled to the
others to enter. We waited. As they entered through the door,
now opened wide, they formed a straight line in order to cover
the entire structure with their firepower. What followed next still
gives me nightmares. As the soldiers rushed into the house, their
legs and bodies got pierced by the spikes and they let out
blood-curdling screams, calling out to their mothers and each
other. One or two even fired their guns without aim and the

bullets whizzed by us. We were momentarily frozen with fright but the flying bullets galvanized us into action. We took aim and as planned earlier, sprayed our bullets into the vague figures at two different angles. The logic was that even if we missed their vitals, we would at least shatter their legs incapacitating them for any further pursuit. After the initial burst, we paused only long enough to insert new magazines and waited for any reaction. There was none; so we quietly slid through a break in the bamboo wall at the rear and ran. We ran and ran downhill until our breath stopped and our hearts refused to beat any more. We rested for a while and groped our way across a stream to the other side and waited there until dawn. Throughout, neither of us said anything but we both knew that we were thinking the same thing: to go back and see what damage we had done in the night.

When the eastern sky lightened, it was Imli who voiced our thoughts. He simply rose from the ground and said, 'Let's go' and without saying anything, I followed him. This time we chose to approach the farmhouse from the direction of the wooded area, which would lead us to the back of the structure. We made our way cautiously, halting every ten minutes or so to check for signs of other patrols or even movements or sounds from within the farmhouse. There were none. In the meantime it was almost daybreak, so we increased our pace and crept on all fours towards the silent derelict structure. We waited, but there seemed to be no sign of life. So we stood up cautiously and peeped through the chinks in the bamboo wall. Five bodies lay sprawled on the mud floor now turned black with their blood. We turned to each other with shock and disbelief. The bodies lay near the threshold of the dilapidated structure at grotesquely twisted angles. We were shocked by the grisly scene and could not at first absorb the fact that we had done that. We crept in through the same hole through which we had fled the previous night and when we went closer, we saw that the bamboo spikes had pierced their bodies at different places, instantly incapacitating them so that our bullets had found sitting ducks. Slowly the enormity of what we had done was beginning sink in and I felt dizzy. Just then, one of the figures, lying a little behind the others, moved a little and moaned. It was apparent that the spike had only gone into his shoulder and because he was not in direct range of our fire, his injuries had not killed him instantly. But he had lost a lot of blood and would soon die. Without a moment's hesitation, I lifted my gun and shot him in the head. After ascertaining that they were all dead, we began to collect their arms and whatever ammunition they had. In the process I had to turn a body, which had fallen on his gun and in so doing, saw the face of the soldier. He was my age and the look of pain and horror on his face seemed so real that I rushed out and vomited. Imli had to extract his gun because I could not go into the hut again. The scavenging completed, we pulled the structure down and set it on fire. Our haul was heavy but we had to leave the area quickly, so we walked as fast as we could not only for our safety but also to get away from the scene of the horrible massacre perpetrated by us. And do you know? We were not yet sixteen when we became such ruthless killers.'

The old man seemed to falter here; the grandson peered closer and saw that he was crying silently. So he poured another cup of tea and offered it to his grieving grandfather. The young boy did not understand why he should be crying; after all they were enemy soldiers, weren't they? But he dared not say anything and waited for the old man to resume his story.

'As luck or ill luck would have it,' the old man started once more, 'we were captured by a patrol of the underground army who had come to the area to ambush a convoy, which was supposed to be coming with supplies for the troops. But it turned out that a bridge had been damaged and so the entire convoy had returned to their base in the plains. They were, however, very happy to relieve us of the arms and ammunition that we had looted and took us once more to a camp in the jungle. The camp commander wanted to know how we came to "procure" the guns. When we told them what we had done, at first he laughed and looking at our faces, said that we were lying. But then he recognized the arms as army issue and also the small rear-guard scout party, which had just returned, confirmed our story by saying that they had seen a farmhouse burning. He grudgingly admitted that there might be some truth in our story. And so he concluded that if the soldiers were indeed dead, the army would surely retaliate by launching an all-out campaign to hunt down the perpetrators; so once more Imli and I found ourselves marching deep into the jungle, this time with an unfriendly and suspicious group.

We stayed with this group for almost a year and went on several ambush missions. Sometimes we would go to intimidate unfriendly villagers by firing in the air in the vicinity of the village and instilling fear into their hearts, we would come away with much needed supplies for the group: sacks of rice, livestock and, on a few occasions, toiletries too. I remember a particular mission, when we inflicted heavy casualties on a small convoy of four or five jeeps. We had taken positions on two opposite hillocks through which the narrow road passed. As soon as the vehicles entered this passage, we sprayed them with bullets from both sides of the road before any of the bodyguards could even take up their weapons. I do not know how many soldiers died or if anyone survived the assault at all. Such details were becoming increasingly irrelevant to our way of thinking and it was only when our side suffered casualties that we thought of the dead and the wounded. Within a short period of time, Imli and I had become hard-core rebels though we never thought of ourselves in those terms at all.

Our group never stayed in one location for long and we shifted camps regularly. I remember our last mission because it was there that my leg was injured. It was an important mission and except for the cook, the entire group was involved. We were to attack a convoy, which was supposed to include some of the interim Naga leaders who were negotiating a permanent settlement within the framework of the Constitution of India. The underground leadership considered this move as a betrayal of the Naga Cause and decided to 'take action' against these traitors by mounting a series of ambushes along the route of the convoy. The attacks were to be carried by different groups, of which we were going to be the advance group. If we failed, others would be waiting further along the way. However, anticipating such a move, the authorities had sent patrolling parties all along the route to ensure maximum security for the convoy. We ran into one such party even before we reached our vantage point. A gun battle followed and realizing that we were terribly outnumbered, we were ordered to run into the jungle to seek shelter. Imli and I too began to run, but before we could reach tree cover, a stray bullet hit me from behind and I went down in a heap. As I fell to the ground, I shouted to Imli to leave me and run to safety. In response, he simply caught the straps of my rucksack and dragged me down a steep incline where we hid for the night. In the morning, he went looking for our comrades, some of whom were dead, and the others either injured or hiding in the jungle. In desperation he trekked to a nearby farm and persuaded a terrified villager to come and help him carry me to our hideout. It took us the best part of the day, but we eventually made it there. The villager was, however, not allowed to enter the perimeter and was sent off with warnings of dire consequences to the entire village if he ever spoke about this to anyone.

The wound on my leg festered and it became obvious that unless I received proper medical attention, gangrene would set in and I would die. It was Imli who proposed that he would go to Mokokchung and negotiate our surrender so that my injury could be treated properly. At first our commander was reluctant, but when Imli pointed out that he would approach the pastor first and request him to be the mediator, he saw that it was a reasonable plan. After some hesitation, he allowed Imli to make the necessary arrangements and after depositing our weapons and taking an oath never to reveal anything about our activities, we left our jungle life forever.

Along the way, some villagers helped us with food and even some pain killers for my swollen leg when they saw my condition. It took us three whole days to reach the pastor's house and by that time I had given up all hope of recovery. My wound had begun to smell, my body was beginning to swell and I slipped into unconsciousness several times on the way. When the pastor saw my condition, he immediately borrowed a contractor's jeep and took me to the civil hospital where an operation took place immediately. The bullet that hit me had made a clean exit but in the process had damaged some vital nerve points and the muscles around them, which had to be removed. The doctor told them that because of this, I would always walk with a limp and there would be intermittent spasms of pain. But he assured them that I would live. It seems that I did not wake up from the anesthesia for two whole days and Imli used to say that it was the only time in his life that he experienced real fear. But I recovered only to find that both Imli and I had to spend some time in the jail because we had taken up arms against the government of India and had to pay the price.

Yes, my dear boy, we did pay the price, but the prison term was the least of it. We came back to the village as it was being reconstructed on the ancient site. But by then many of our age were dead, as was Imli's father, some were maimed like me, and Toshi and many others had drifted away to live on the fringes of society unable to lead normal lives because of the trauma suffered during our careers as freedom fighters. If I have survived and seem normal, it is because of the love and friendship of Imli and the devotion of your grandmother who understood my secret pain and sustained me with her unquestioning love. Our youth was claimed by the turbulence, which transformed boys, like Imli and me into killers. Yes, we did kill many people but the truth is that till today I cannot say how I feel about that, which sometimes makes me wonder if I have turned into a monster. However, among the many secrets that your grandfather Imli and I shared, what I have just revealed to you was the most painful to bear because it was a constant reminder of our lost youth.'

But there was another secret, he was saying to himself, which Imli and I shared. The recollection of that incident never failed to fill him with awe and wonder because it took him back to his innocent boyhood. Even now, he could see the bouncing breasts and the darkness below of the young woman, walking

tall in broad daylight. And another throught occurred to him
only then: he and Imli had been so busy staring at certain areas
of her anatomy that they never once glanced at her face and
therefore they had remained ignorant of her identity! His wife's
explanation years later, was a practical one: the human body was
not a subject for speculation or abstraction. The act of walking
naked while the woman's clothes dried did not seem to his wife
anything out of the ordinary. Old man Sashi now thought to
himself that he should have been telling his grandson about this
secret and chuckling over the 'man-talk' but instead, he found
himself explaining to him about that area of darkness in his life,
which he had tried so hard to wish away.

His ruminations over, he continued, 'He used to tell me,
"Sashi, we owe it to them, and since you are a better story teller,
you tell them." I did not agree with him, thinking that what
happened to us then would be of no relevance to the young of the
land now who have not carried a load on their heads and cannot
go to the next village if there is no vehicle. But I was wrong and
I admit that now. I had to tell you this because it is the secret of
out lost youth and also because I realise that once in a lifetime one
ought to face the truth. Truth about the self, the land and above
all, the truth about history. I do not know if what I have just told
you answers your question or makes you understand your reasons
for asking it. But there is nothing more I can add. You have to
make what you can from what I have tried to tell you.'

So saying he went out to the bamboo platform at the back of
the house. Moa remained seated at the low stool near the
fireplace. He heard his grandfather clear his throat, blow his nose
and pass water noisily and then silence. He turned his head
towards the platform, but could not see the old man because the
lingering darkness of the departing night hid him from view. So
he got up and went to see what his grandfather was doing. He
found him standing on the edge of the platform, looking at the
bank of white clouds shrouding the valley below, deep in thought.
Moa went near him and stood by his side. They heard cocks
crowing in the distance and by and by saw faint lights in

some houses. Life was stirring in the village. Their silhouettes were becoming dearer as darkness was giving way to a misty haze. Sensing the grandson's presence, old man Sashi put his arms around the young boy's shoulder and turned his face towards the eastern sky now brightening with the light of a new dawn. And the earth continued to be.

The Journey

The squealing of a piglet which escaped to the main room where they were sleeping awakened the young girl. It was still dark but she was already alert because this was the day that she was returning to her boarding school. The winter vacation of nearly two months seemed to have gone by very quickly and she was feeling a little disturbed at the prospect of having to undergo another drastic change of environment. She still remembered clearly each detail of the journey which had brought her from the plains of Assam to her village in the Naga Hills. After the journey from her school to the foothill town of Mariani, she had spent the night in the loft of a kindly shopkeeper. In the morning she saw the women of the group cooking rice and curry, enough for two meals—one to eat before they set out, and another to be eaten at noon when they reached the half-way point of their journey. The rice that was cooked came from each member of the party because it was the custom for villagers to carry sufficient provisions which would last them for their journey. A large common pot, big enough to cook for the group was carried by one member and every time they had to prepare a meal, each one put in a cupful of rice from the store of rations they carried.

After a cold and restless night, the young girl was hungry and ate voraciously. She wondered if her brother, too, had brought provisions or if he had worked out some other arrangement with a distant cousin who was with this particular group. The firewood required for cooking meals had been gathered at the, foothills before the start of the journey. After the morning meal, the party set off at a brisk pace in single file; every member's basket laden with salt, dry fish, soap, bottles of hair oil and even kerosene oil for the lamps. These were purchased with the money they earned by selling oranges, ginger, yam and at times special sticky rice. Such journeys were possible only during the winter months because the many hill streams and rivers that criss-crossed the terrain could only be traversed when the water level was down, just knee deep at points. The villages would cross in groups, holding one another's hands so that they did not get swept away by the swift currents.

It was one such group that her brother had teamed up with when he came to escort her from her school to the village. The early start ensured that the travellers would reach home before sunset. She remembered again how her brother, walking behind her, would urge her to walk faster, telling her, 'Faster, faster, in the evenings tigers roam these jungles'. In spite of the fearful prospect, she could not keep pace with the others and when they reached the half-way mark on the banks of the Disoi river, the others were waiting impatiently for their arrival. Some had even opened their leaf packets of rice and curry, ready to start as soon as everyone arrived. Some women from the group came over to the young girl and dropped some pieces of meat on her leaf plate. As a result, she had a huge mound of rice and many pieces of meat which she could not finish. When she was about to throw away the leftover food, her brother scolded her, 'Don't do that, pack up everything and carry it in your bag.' After they had eaten, they entered the river. The water was knee deep for the adults but reached up to her eyebrows! Her brother and another man hoisted her up, each putting his hand under an armpit and safely carrying her to the other bank.

Soon after crossing the river, the road became steep, at first gradually but from a certain point, almost perpendicular. It was more than the girl could negotiate and she sat down on one of the stone steps and began to cry. The others had already gone quite far ahead, so they did not see this. But the brother was worried, he sat down with her for a while and soothed her, pointing to the sun moving towards the west and telling her once again of the dangers lurking in the jungle. He could not carry her even if he had wanted to; he was carrying her tin trunk with a few of her belongings inside. She remembered how she struggled over every step until, when the sun had almost set, they reached the village. When she woke up the next morning her feet were swollen enormously and for one whole week she could not walk properly.

Now on this morning when she would have to make the same journey again, cross the same river, and travel further either by train or bus to her boarding school, she was full of misgivings. The racket created by the piglet had awakened her aunt and she was trying to prod the huddled figures wrapped in torn blankets asleep on mats on the floor. She got up first and going to her tin case, checked that her favourite dress, which her cousin was eying all winter, was there. In no time at all a simple meal was cooked by her aunt and after eating this, the young girl and her brother stepped out of the house to begin the journey back. Even though it was still dark, it was imperative that they make this early start in order to get a connecting bus or train to her school town.

If the journey up the hill was difficult, she found that climbing down the narrow perpendicular steps cut into the hillside was equally difficult, if not more dangerous. She was wearing a pair of shoes given to her by a senior at the school hostel who was tired of them. This was the first decent pair of shoes she had had since her parents died and she had been sent off to the missionary school to continue her studies there. She was determined to leave the village in style because they were not allowed to wear shoes at school. But she soon realised how difficult it was to walk fast in a pair of shoes a size larger than her feet. So she took them off and tying them together with the laces, strung them around her neck like a garland. They were now dangling at an awkward angle and adding to her woes. Seeing her plight, a kindly woman who was travelling with them offered to carry the shoes in her basket. Tinula was greatly relieved. After what seemed like ages, they reached the plains and the journey became somewhat tolerable. By now the sun was up and its rays were penetrating the thick foliage creating an unbelievably beautiful landscape. She could hear the varied tones of different birds flitting from the branches and calling out to each other. But the travellers had no time to stop and look or listen to anything. They had to keep up a steady pace, especially Tinula and her brother, Temjenba, as they had to reach Mariani by four in the afternoon. At one point, after the party negotiated a puddle by walking over a fallen log, they came across a peculiarly shaped depression and fresh dung near it upon which the rays of the afternoon sun shone directly. Tinula's brother exclaimed to the older woman, 'Aunty, there must be elephants here. Look at the trees, all the bark has been eaten up. And we really have to hurry. We cannot wait here for the elephants to pass.' The woman replied, 'Do not worry nephew, they have already crossed our route. Look at the break in the forest to your left; they have gone to the other side away from our path.' Tinula wondered how the old woman knew this, because, to her, the forest looked the same everywhere.

Just like her journey to the village earlier, they ate their midday meal on the bank of the almost dry river and once again Tinula was helped by her brother and another man to cross the river. When they reached flatter land, the direct rays of the sun began to burn into the young girl's skin making her feel thirsty and itchy. But she had to keep up with the others who had increased their speed. Sometimes she found herself running to catch up with them, afraid that some wild animal would spring out of the forest and devour her.

The winter sun was almost setting when Tinula and her brother reached the railway platform. There was no time to purchase tickets; so they simply jumped onto the train and immediately it chugged out of the station. It was one of those suburban trains which stopped at all kinds of stations, sometimes to take in a single passenger and once or twice it stopped even when there was no one. All this while she and her brother were standing, holding on to the window frames to keep from falling.

After some time Tinula felt a tap on her shoulder; a man was pointing to a small space beside him. She tried to sit but the space was so small that she had to turn sideways to keep her bottom on the hard wooden plank of the seat. No matter, she was grateful for the edge-hold and leaning her head on the wall she began to doze off.

At one of the small stations when the train stopped for a little longer than the earlier stops, Temjenba went out quickly and bought two *singaras* and two 'single' cups of stale tea. 'Single' in tea stall jargon meant half a cup served in a small earthen *kullar* to make it look full. The singara was cold and the tea, too, did not taste like tea at all; but it was some food and Tinula was grateful for that. After what seemed to be an endless jostling and bumping, the train finally stopped at its last station called Farkating. It was the station nearest to the boarding school. From here they had to travel still further to reach it. But it was nearly midnight and the whole station area was deserted. Even the station master was now locking up his little room of an office. Holding up a hurricane lamp, he was looking this way and that to ascertain that everything was in order. Temjenba was greatly worried; how could they walk to the school, a distance of about three or four miles in the middle of a dark winter night? He stood there for some time wondering what to do next when, suddenly out of the darkness, a man approached him asking where they were going. When Temjenba gave the name of the school, the man replied, 'I am going a little farther but will pass by the school. I can drop you and your sister right at the gate of the school.' This seemed like a boon from heaven itself and so, grabbing hold of Tinula's hand, he followed the kind man to a waiting car. In later years Tinula was to realize that the 'big' car in which she and her brother had sat squeezed tightly among the other passengers that night had been an Ambassador.

At the school, her brother first dropped the tin trunk over the top of the gate, then hoisted Tinula over it, and finally jumped in himself. He then proceeded towards the Superintendent's bungalow. After much knocking, the lady herself opened the door to her office. She was annoyed at first for having been awakened at this unearthly hour but when she saw the shivering duo, she quietly went inside and came out with a torch saying to Temjenba, 'You can go now.' He merely nodded at his sister and without a word retraced his steps towards the gate and the dark night.

The Superintendent took Tinula to the school infirmary which was temporarily being used to keep latecomers overnight after the holidays. Since there was no extra bed that night, she was allowed to share the one in which her friend, Winnie, was sleeping. Tinula washed her feet as best as she could and crept into the warmth of the bed where, very grudgingly, Winnie made some space for her. She was struck immediately by not only the warmth of the bed after her cold and long journey but also by the softness of the sheets. She was suddenly reminded of her last night in the village when she had had to fight for her share of the tattered blanket with her cousins, and how she was awakened by the squealing of the piglet in the early morning. The transition from that environment to this one seemed so abrupt and incongruous that Tinula began to giggle to herself. This annoyed Winnie so much that she shouted 'Shut up' in a loud voice provoking the housemother to scold them both, telling them to go to sleep quietly. For a while, they kept quiet; and just when Tinula was about to fall asleep in the cozy fold of the soft blanket with a warm body next to hers, Winnie said to her out of the blue, 'You know your boyfriend, Hubert, has a new girlfriend now.' The announcement was so sudden and so out of context that Tinula was taken completely by surprise. She was just thirteen and to call Hubert a 'boyfriend' was, of course, fanciful thinking. They had merely exchanged 'looks' at church a few times, but being an outgoing sort of person Tinula had once or twice mentioned his name and said that she found him 'nice'. In her heart of hearts she knew that nothing would come of this fancy but, secretly, she did hope that he too had noticed her. The suddenness and the tone in which Winnie said the words hurt her deeply, and in order to camouflage her real emotions, Tinula started to giggle again until tears came to her eyes and the giggles began to sound like muffled sobs. Winnie lay inert on her side while the girl next to her continued heaving. She wondered momentarily whether she was laughing or crying, but she really did not care.

Today, if you ask her, Tinula cannot tell you with any certainty whether she laughed or cried herself to sleep that night but it was a night that stayed with her as the defining moment of a great transition. In many ways the journey from her village to the school was traumatic enough but the veiled antipathy of Winnie's remark made her realise that the barriers of life are not only the physical ones. If she felt any disappointment or even a little bit of jealousy when she was told that a boy that she liked had found a new 'girlfriend', she does not recall. What she recalls today is the deliberate attempt to hurt revealed by the tone in which the news was broken to her. She had always considered Winnie a good friend and was happy to meet her after the holidays. But now she realized that a strange emotion had overtaken her and was forcing her to look at the warm body lying next to her in a different way. She wanted to leave the bed and go somewhere else. But it was late and the Superintendent had gone back to her room. Besides, what reason could she give for her request to sleep elsewhere? So she simply turned her back and pretended to sleep, though her body continued to shake for a long while.

Once in a while she wonders vaguely about what happened to a boy called Hubert whom she had never met face to face. But she often remembers a girl called Winnie and that unforgettable winter night, the girl who forced a thirteen-year-old girl to embark on a different kind of journey.

A New Chapter

Gradually the earth seemed to be settling down, as though after a protracted period of violent storms that had ripped through her heart. Life in the village seemed to regain some semblance of normality. People were talking of sowing and planting crops in the fields as in the old days before the upheavals. With fresh hope in their hearts, they were also talking of re-building burnt down homes and granaries. Schoolchildren were seen rummaging through the rubble of their homes to see if any book could be salvaged as school buildings were now being repaired so that classes could begin. Women were retrieving their weaving tools hidden away in jungle storage places in order to begin weaving much-needed cloth for their families. Menfolk examined their cutting implements, honing them on sandy whetstones. They were preparing to begin clearing the forest of young shrubs for the next *jhum*. They knew that the job would not be as difficult as in the old days because the scorched earth had not yet had enough time to replenish herself; the vegetation was young and consisted only of tender saplings, which could be cleared without much effort. In the old days such areas would have been allowed to lie fallow for at least nine or ten years before the cycle was resumed. But the core of the earth had changed forever in the last decade and they had no choice but to turn to her ravaged body, to hurt her some more and extract whatever she could yield to them from her depleted resources.

It was the mid-sixties in Nagaland and an uneasy surface calm prevailed. People were beginning to take stock of what had so suddenly overturned their quiet lives and changed every single man or woman in the land forever. Slowly and painfully Nagas were beginning to look at themselves through new prisms, some self-created and some thrust upon them. Those who survived, learnt to adopt to the new trends and new lifestyles. Old loyalties became suspect as new players emerged and forged makeshift alliances in unfamiliar political spaces. But the battle lines remained the same; the forces merely shifted their vantage points and re-invented their strategies to accommodate the new equations. While the underground forces retreated further into their jungle hideouts, the occupying army ensconced itself in prime locations in towns and villages and built new fortified homes away from home. Life in these enclaves appeared more or less normal, but every now and then rumours of sophisticated weaponry being stealthily brought into certain strategic locations during night curfew would float around. However, after the initial fear and apprehension everyone would fall back into their 'normal' routine of life. In the upper circles of society, the rumour that the bigwigs were planning to add new recreational facilities like a billiards table in the club and a golf course for the officers in the Army Headquarters, created a temporary flurry of excitement among those who hoped to enter that charmed circle. But when nothing came of this particular rumour, it was back to business as usual.

But in order to justify the presence of the armed forces who were in danger of their very lives in the 'troubled' area (not to speak of the many perks they enjoyed for the 'punishment posting'), it was necessary for them to have 'encounters' with the rebel groups. These were sometimes genuine but more often, not. The countryside would ring out with loud explosions and then reports would filter in with inflated casualty figures and announcements of capturing either members of the rebel groups or arms and ammunition from their camps. Whatever be the truth, the army was here to stay and they had to be housed and fed in a proper manner.

It was to procure 'supplies' for these army establishments that a new class quickly emerged. They came to be known as army contractors who now entered the space between the opposing factions and were poised to make their fortunes from the spoils of war. They were often persons with 'connections' in the right places, both overground and underground. They became the new factor in the hierarchy now evolving in Naga society in the wake of the upheaval. These people had easy access to the army high command and enjoyed privileges not available to ordinary civilians. For example, they could purchase things from the Brigade canteen whenever they liked including liquor at subsidised army rates. They got invited to army and government parties and functions and were treated at par with both army and civil officers. In short, these contractors were actually a new class of Nagas, who emerged as the third force in the power equation between the two warring armies. Both sides recognised their utility in their game and used them unscrupulously.

Even among the contractors, it was the ones with big money who bagged the headquarter contracts, while the second grade ones had to content themselves with the outpost contracts. The latter had to travel to all the outputs of the army and paramilitary forces with the 'contracted' supplies on designated days in the week. When supplies from the plains did not reach them on time, they scoured the adjoining villages for vegetables, livestock and other items so that they could fulfil the terms of their contract. Among this group of contractors there was a man called Bendangnungsang who found himself plying this trade because he could not complete his college education and did not want to settle for a clerical job in the government. He came from a good family; all his brothers and sisters held high government posts and he decided that if he could not be a 'sahib' like his siblings, he would be the moneymaker of the family.

But his pretensions of being a big player in the money market were not backed by any understanding or practical experience of 'making' money. He started his business with capital borrowed from his father and began to travel in the jeep that he owned, towing a trailer full of supplies for the outposts. Several times he had to go to his own village to procure vegetables and livestock to supply to outposts near the village. In the course of such business trips, he got reacquainted with a distant cousin of his who had a vegetable farm. This woman was a widow with two small children. Since there was no man in the family, she was unable to cultivate rice because this involved heavy work. That is how she came to have her field of vegetables which became her sole means of earning a livelihood. After a year or two of doing this, she decided to rear pigs as well. There was a practical reason for this decision. Each time a crop of vegetables was sold, there would be a mound of old leftover vegetables, unfit for selling, which had to be thrown away. When neighbours started scrambling for these scraps to feed their animals, she began to think of starting a piggery herself. But she had to wait a few more years for her financial situation to improve so that she could ask her brothers to help her build the sty and accompany her to the nearby village to buy piglets. It was a struggle, but her efforts were rewarded within two years. The twin ventures were complementary: the pigs were reared on the unsaleable vegetables while the vegetables thrived beautifully on manure supplied by the animals. Life had started to get just a wee bit more comfortable for the widow and her sons.

When Nungsang, as everyone called him, came to the village looking for supplies, he opened a new market for Merenla's produce. Apart from buying vegetables, he also brought a few pigs from her, for which he paid in cash. Seeing how much they needed each other's business, Nungsang began to advise her on the kind of vegetables she should cultivate. He even bought seeds for her when any new vegetable was introduced in the farm.

But things were not working out as well as Nungsang had thought. He discovered that the approved rates of his contract were often at par with what he paid his suppliers and sometimes even higher because he had to keep to his commitment and make his deliveries on time. Also, the items had to be in strict compliance with the terms of the contract. After the first six months, he realised that he was not making any profit at all. He was in a real quandary; all his dreams of making easy money were evaporating right before his eyes as he delivered live goats and pigs, called 'meat-on-hoof' in contract parlance, at an increasing loss. The fish that came from the plains often rotted before delivery and got rejected as a result. There were times when carton after carton of fruit had to be thrown away because their contents were in less than perfect condition. If he continued in this fashion, his business would be wiped out even before completing the first year. And all his secret dreams of competing for the prime Headquarter supplies contract would remain just that. Now he would have to borrow more money to payoff the mounting debts owed to the petty suppliers whom he had to beg and cajole to let him have their goods on credit. Nungsang realized that he had to somehow dig himself out of this hole if he hoped to compete for next year's contract. He knew that there was a method to this. His friends in the same trade seemed to be making good money while he found himself on the verge of being wiped out in the very first year of his contract. He decided to swallow his pride and ask one of them the secret of his success.

The person he decided to approach was simply known as Bhandari and his was an extraordinary story of achievement. He belonged to a community that had been given land in the town in recognition of their service to the British army during the great wars. His grandfather had been rewarded thus, as were many others who raised generations of families in the alien land, which had now become their 'home'. This man had started out as a handyman in a rich man's household, learnt to drive and was soon driving for him. Within a few years he bought an old jeep, left his job and began to travel to the plains to bring supplies for the shopkeepers in town. After some time he bought a secondhand Land Rover for himself from a tea planter and hired a driver to take him around. This vehicle was his most prized possession— no one was allowed to touch it. In his usual uncouth way, he would joke that asking for his Rover, even for a few hours, was more offensive than borrowing his wife for the night! When the army contract boom began, he became one of the first to bag the prestigious Headquarter contract and seemed to be doing extremely well. Nungsang and he had been drinking and card-playing cronies for many years now and it was to him that the hapless contractor turned for advice and tips on how to turn his business around.

The very next evening Nungsang went to his house. Bhandari had been engaged in this new business for barely five or six years but he was obviously doing very well. His children were now studying in boarding schools in Shillong and he had also constructed a new R.C.C. building in place of his old home. After the initial inanities, Nungsang brought out the bottle of Scotch he had brought and they sat down to an evening of 'paploo' with some other cronies who were already there. Throughout the evening, Bhandari noticed that Nungsang was restless, he did not seem to be enjoying his drink nor was he really interested in the card game. Sensing that his friend was in trouble, he managed to send away the others saying that he had to discuss something important with his friend. After the others left he asked Nungsang what was troubling him. Bhandari listened to his friend's tale of woe and, smiling cryptically, said, 'All you educated people are such bloody fools'. Then, he continued in Hindi, *'Tumlog bahut imandari dikhane mangta hai aur* contract *me jo likha hai wohi deta hai, na?'* Nungsang was dumbfounded. He exclaimed, 'What do you mean?' Bhandari merely gave him a pitying look and brought out pen and paper. He made two columns and began to write. Parallel to the approved items, he put the names of alternatives; for example, in the place of meat-on-hoof he wrote pumpkins, squash and gourd. For fresh fish, he indicated dried fish; in place of apples and mangoes he wrote pears and plums, available in abundance locally during the season. Nungsang was dumbfounded; he said that the N.C.O. in-charge would never accept these substitutions. Bhandari clicked his tongue in exasperation and again spoke in Hindi, (he had studied only up to class VI and did not speak much English) *'Aare, budhu, tum kya sochta hai? Yeh* tender *ka* item officer *logo ke liye hai, aur baki chize jawano ke liye. Yeh jo mera ghar bana he na,* meat-on-hoof *se nahi, kadu lauki se bana.'* Nungsang was still skeptical, how would be convince the Subedar Major to accept substitutes for the genuine articles? Seeing the naivete and helplessness on Nungsang's face, Bhandari offered to accompany him on his next supply trip to the outpost.

On the appointed day, the two contractors carried a bottle of Scotch and a roasted chicken. Before the supplies were unloaded, Bhandari introduced himself and invited the N.C.O. to sit down for a drink and a chat. It so happened that this man was from Bhandari's own community and immediately a bond was struck. They began to speak in their own language; at first the other man seemed to be protesting but eventually he seemed to calm down and a deal was struck. For a considered sum, he would accept substitutes twice a month, but he also cautioned them that if the fraud ever came to light he would plead ignorance and say that he was coerced into accepting the unauthorized items. Mission accomplished, the supplies were unloaded, the invoices duly certified and signed, and the two friends left the camp after shaking hands with the slightly dazed officer.

A different phase of business thus began for this new entrant to the field. He began to buy more pumpkins than livestock and the local vegetable and fruit sellers began to bring their produce to his doorstep, vying with each other for his trade. By the financial year-end, he managed to break even and the new year's contract was once again awarded to him. The list of substitutes now included dry fish also. So he went to a dry fish wholesaler named Abdul Sattar, who had a stall in the new market recently constructed by the Town Committee, and made a deal with him. Nungsang would make an initial deposit of Rs 2,000 and he would be able to take other consignments on credit until he received his monthly payment. So in place of fresh fish, the outpost jawans had to eat the stinking dry fish twice a month. Of course, the officers in the same camp got their normal quota of fresh meat and fish throughout the month.

When he visited the village after a gap of a few months, he discovered that Merenla's pigs had grown quite big; so he bought two of them and supplied them to the camp because it was Durga Puja time and he could not risk the prospect of the jawans' complaints by depriving them of their favourite meat during the festivities. Nungsang was becoming 'savvy' in the ways of the world and began to make a good profit through this network of fraudulent substitution. Emboldened by the success of this, he began to manipulate the contract in other ways too. When he first began his supply business, he was very prompt in paying his various suppliers on time. But now he stopped doing this and it was only when their frequent visits to the house became a source of friction with his wife that he would dole out the payments, sometimes only half of what he owed, and threaten them that he would take his business to others who would not pester him so. He actually did this to Abdul Sattar, the dry fish dealer, because one day he refused to accept a part payment and said that if Sahib did not clear his account, he would complain to the Town Committee Chairman. Nungsang became incensed and abused him and almost threw him out of the house. The next day he went to the market and negotiated terms with another dealer named Karim who had a stall right next to Sattar's. It was his way of showing him what he could do to those who objected to his capricious business dealings. The fruit seller who sold him mangoes and bananas, which Nungsang supplied for the officers, was not paid anything for months on end, though he had on two occasions tried to meet him at home, unsuccessfully. After seeing what happened to Sattar, no one now dared to ask the contractor for payment. Right before their eyes, this member of a prestigious family of the town, who seemed so decent and friendly in the beginning was turning out to be a common bully. Not only would he not clear his outstanding bills, he would insist on taking more stuff on contract from them with veiled threats of dire consequences. These petty traders had no choice but to endure the injustice because Nungasang's brother-in-law was a First Class Magistrate in the Deputy Commissioner's office who could instantly cancel their Inner Line Permits on some pretext or the other and then they would be thrown out of the town.

While this was the reality behind Nungsang's apparent success as a contractor, hidden eyes in the jungle were closely monitoring his comings and goings along with the other contractors. The cost of the new weaponry needed to combat the Indian army was enormous and the 'collections' from the general population were nowhere near the mark. The supposed lucre of this new band of players in the emerging economic front presented itself as a new source of 'revenue' for them. They had already extracted sizeable sums from the headquarter contractors. Nungsang somehow got wind of this and began to plan a counter move. Through his contacts he learned that the area commander of the region where he plied his trade was an old high school classmate. He sent word through the grapevine that he wished to meet him. On the appointed day, which happened to be a regular supply day, Nungsang finished his job in the outpost earlier than usual and on the return trip, took his jeep into a disused road and waited patiently. Towards dusk, hearing stealthy footsteps he became alert and, at the same time, a bit anxious wondering if he had made a mistake in trying to manipulate these people and whether he had landed himself in real danger. As he was thinking these thoughts, suddenly, out of nowhere, half a dozen armed men surrounded his jeep and motioned for him to step out. In the dim twilight he could not make out their features, but he had the distinct impression that the soldiers were very young. After a little while, his old classmate Wati came out of the shadows and solemnly the two shook hands. He then dismissed his guards who melted away into the gathering darkness but Nungsang knew that they would be keeping vigil from previously selected vantage points. Left alone, these two old friends became more relaxed, Nungsang brought out a bottle of Scotch and two glasses and they began to discuss 'business'. He tried to convince the commander that his business was not doing as well as that of the town contractors and that if he had to pay the underground outfit the same percentage, he would be totally ruined. Couldn't the classmate suggest a way out? At first the wily jungle man would not commit himself to anything. Nungsang continued to plead his case. When the booze hit the halfway mark, the other man began to ask the contractor about his brothers and sisters. Nungsang immediately sensed that there was a catch somewhere in the inquiry because the underground outfit knew everything about everybody in town, especially those in government service. However, he went along with the other's ploy and gave all the details of his siblings and where they were posted. The jungle man began with the preamble that he himself could not do anything about condoning Nungsang's 'dues' to his government, but there might be a way to work out a deal if he promised to do something important for his boss. He then went on to explain that the boss's eldest son was a college dropout and was becoming a nuisance to his mother in town. If he were inducted as a clerk in any government department, his boss would be eternally grateful to Nungsang and he would then ensure that the underground 'tax collectors' would not bother him as long as he and his boss remained in-charge of the area. It seemed that even in the parallel 'government' set-up of the underground, transfers of 'officers' were a routine policy matter.

Nungsang was taken aback. This line of negotiation had never occurred to him and now he began to think fast. He said that since the authorities in Nagaland knew the names of all the bigwigs in the underground, it might be difficult to find a job for the son of his boss. The other man quickly countered this by saying that the father's name could be changed and better still, the name of his village, too, could be changed. The discussion went on for some time until Nungsang came up with the suggestion: why not send the son to Assam where one of his brothers, the older one in the Border Areas Department, and the other in the Police, could find him a placement? The other man thought for a while and agreed to place this suggestion before his boss. Before parting, Nungsang brought out another bottle of liquor and handed it to his classmate along with a carton of cigarettes and some bundles of 'bidi'. The jungle man simply nodded his thanks and walked away telling Nungsang that he should expect to hear back within the week.

Business continued as usual for Nungsang. He continued to supply his lowly vegetables in place of 'meat-on-hoof' twice a month having successfully carried off this trick so far, even three times one month! But the Subedar Major put his foot down and the wily contractor was forced to fall in line. Two weeks had already passed since his meeting in the jungle, yet there was no news from his classmate. Meanwhile stories of forcible 'tax collections' not only from townspeople but also from villagers were being heard more frequently. On his next visit to the village, he found Merenla in a dejected state. She told him that one day a gang of armed men had entered their village and taken away large quantities of rice and other foodstuff from several houses in the village including livestock like goats and pigs, her prize sow being the biggest among them. Angrily, she added that one of the men had laughed when he saw her pumpkins on the bamboo platform in the back of the house and that before leaving he had smashed a few with his rifle butt saying, 'Let this be your meat aunty, ours have four legs'. By way of consoling her Nungsang bought the rest of the pumpkins and paid her in cash. Walking away from her house, he somehow felt good that he was able to do a good turn to someone in distress. On his way to town, he unloaded the consignment in the outpost despite the protests of the Subedar Major who complained that his whole camp was beginning to smell of rotten pumpkins now. Nungsang ignored him and went on his way. He was driving slowly, lost in thought, when suddenly some young boys appeared in the middle of the road and ordered him to stop. He was frightened. Though the boys wore ordinary clothes, there was a different air about the way they stood and looked at him. After parking his jeep on the side of the road, Nungsang got down and, as calmly as he could, asked them what the matter was. They simply motioned for him to walk towards a jungle path, one leading the way and the others following behind. After about fifteen minutes or so, they came to a secluded spot in the bush where Nungsang saw his classmate. As soon as the scouts were dismissed, the other man told Nungsang that his boss had agreed to his suggestion, but that he did not want his son to join any security force, police or otherwise. Nungsang explained that the matter might take some months and that the young boy should report to him immediately so that he could be sent to

Shillong to await his appointment. After settling this deal and assuring Nungsang that he would not be bothered about 'taxes' the jungle man brought out a gift for his classmate: a special kind of fish found only in a certain river in the Ao territory, cooked in a bamboo container. Nungsang was deeply touched and thanked him profusely. This fish had become a rarity now as all the rivers had been indiscriminately bombed or bleached to catch them. He had often described the exotic taste of this fish to his wife but she refused to believe him until she tasted it herself. Now, here was an opportunity to prove to her that he was not exaggerating.

Nungsang had been anticipating a meeting of this kind when no message had come to him for weeks. So in order to be prepared for such an eventuality, he had kept a parcel for his classmate in the jeep. It contained two pairs of jungle boots, woollen vests and stockings, insect repellants and the inevitable liquor and cigarettes. After saying goodbye to his classmate, he asked the scouts to follow him to the jeep and sent the package to the waiting man in the jungle. Carrying the fish cooked in a bamboo container, he started his jeep and proceeded towards town and home. While the immediate problem of paying 'taxes' to the leader had been held off, he knew that he had to invoke filial loyalties in the strongest terms if he were to succeed in keeping his part of the bargain. He had to somehow convince his father first, for only through his influence would his brother agree to such a deal. He knew his own family and was confident that though there would be the initial shocked response, they would come through for him, because he was considered to be the odd one out who had missed his opportunities in life and in their own individual ways, they all felt sorry for him. As he had anticipated, his father was at first furious: how could he commit himself to such a treacherous deal with the underground people? What would his brother say? Had he forgotten that they were all government servants? He flatly refused to do anything about the proposition and stopped talking to the son for one whole week but Nungsang worked on his mother's sentiments. Though he knew that there was no immediate danger to him because both he and his classmate had agreed that finding a berth for the boy in any government office would take time, he pretended otherwise and stayed at home saying that he was afraid to go out on his usual business trips. He knew that his mother would panic because there were enough instances of people being killed for failing to comply with the demands of the underground and no one was immune to the general fear psychosis. This factor and the mother's constant allusions to the threat to her son's life finally overcame the proud government pensioner's resistance. Though plagued by a sense of guilt, the reluctant father allowed the boy to be sent to his eldest son and wrote a letter saying that unless he found a job for him, his younger brother would face dire consequences. The brother, too, was thus drawn into the manipulation and with the help of a fellow officer, the boy was appointed a clerk in another department after having to wait for two months. Nungsang was greatly relieved but it never occurred to him to even think for a moment what it must have cost his father to make this compromise nor what his brother had to do to procure the job. Only years later when Nungsang heard that the clerk, now a head assistant, was married to his classmate's daughter, he thought to himself that he was not the only manipulator.

Though the business was now 'picking up', thanks to the various manipulations he had become an expert at, the years of being a mere contractor were beginning to take a toll on Nungsang. Though he still hobnobbed with people like Bhandari, he had always harboured notions of his own superiority over people like him who came from nondescript backgrounds. He began to dream of a better future: he decided that haggling with dry fish dealers and fruit vendors and going to the appalling livestock 'mahals' to buy the twice-monthly rations of 'meat-on-hoof' was not going to be his permanent vocation in life. Bhandari and his kind could keep all such contracts for all he cared. But for Nungsang, the son of a prestigious family, there had to be something much higher than this work, which he increasingly thought of as demeaning and much below his status. Why, he said to himself, he was no better than the Abdul Sattars and Karims of the world! But the question was, what else could he do? With this inner dissatisfaction distracting him all the time, he began to drink more, became irritable at home and even more belligerent with the foolhardy creditors who came to the house to press for payment and were unceremoniously chased off the premises with abusive words ringing in their ears. The only consolation he had was that in spite of his growing dissatisfaction with his trade, he was able to build a decent house for his family on a plot of land given to him by his father. Outwardly, of course, Nungsang was his old swaggering self at parties, drinking hard and at times boasting about his family background. The parties that he threw at home were becoming more boisterous and sometimes he went to the extent of saying that he had the most beautiful wife in town as if that was a 'qualification' of sorts, much to the mortification of the young girl he had married, who was aware of his inner turmoil.

In the meantime, the political affiliations in the state were veering away from the idealists. Nagaland had become a state of the Indian union, the first Legislative Assembly was in place and it became apparent that Nagaland was now working its way to becoming a part of the much-vaunted 'mainstream' politics of the country. After two years of his election, an MLA died, creating a vacancy and necessitating a bye-election. This was just the kind of opportunity that Nungsang was looking for. He once again went to Bhandari and broached the subject. At first, Bhandari was simply amused but later dismissive about Nungsang entering the political arena. He said, 'What do you know about politics?' and reverting once again to Hindi, he continued, *'Tumko kaun vote dega? Tumhara party kiya hai? Ruling party ne to aur kisiko chun liya he.'* It was indeed true that Merennungba had already been chosen as the nominee of the party in power and his campaign had been launched with much fanfare only the day before. But Nungsang was adamant. He tried to convince Bhandari that as the new group of influence makers, if they had a representative in the Assembly, they would become more powerful and this would help them gain a stronger foothold in the new economy of the state. This made sense to Bhandari but he was still unsure about Nungsang's candidature. They debated long into the night and recognising the near desperation in his friend's arguments, his long-time crony promised to convene a meeting of all the contractors the next day to enlist their endorsement and financial support.

The meeting, which was held in Bhandari's house, continued till late in the evening. While some people initially made fun of Nungsang's ambition openly, others began to see certain merits in the proposal. Bhandari recited what Nungsang had said in their private meeting the night before as though the idea was his own. Nungsang was at first surprised at the misrepresentation that his wily friend had just uttered but he let it ride because it was going to work in his favour. Bhandari tried to convince his fellow businessmen that they should grab this opportunity of sending one of their own to the seat of power in the state and added that among the contractors there was no better candidate than Nungsang because of his family connections. After some more deliberation, at around ten that night, the contractors adopted a momentous resolution: they would sponsor Nungsang as their candidate for the Assembly and he would run as an independent candidate and if elected, would try to join the ruling party. The big question now was finding the funds. Being businessmen, they decided to approach the business community of the town and raise as much money as they could; the rest, they said, would be the candidate's lookout. In the list of businessmen, they included even the petty shopkeepers and suppliers like Abdul Sattar and Karim. The irony was that Nungsang owed these people considerable sums, but now they found themselves compelled to contribute towards his campaign! They could do nothing about this except pay up. And on such a note a new chapter of this contractor's life began.

The family was, at first, like Bhandari, dismissive about Nungsang's prospects and bluntly refused to have anything to do with a mad-cap venture like running for an Assembly seat, which they thought was already in the pocket of the official candidate. Knowing Nungsang and his limitations they thought that he would not find many supporters even if the funds were somehow managed. But when certain disgruntled sections of the ruling party began to lend covert support to the independent candidate, they too began to have second thoughts and even to secretly relish the prospect of their brother becoming an M.L.A., which was a much more respectable thing than being a mere contractor. The father was initially non-committal; but when he saw the gradual build-up of support for his son, he decided that the family should be actively involved. He told his other children that Nungsang had a real chance of being elected and if that were to happen, it would greatly enhance the family's prestige. Besides, since Nungsang had set his heart on this venture and needed his family's support, each one should contribute towards the campaign fund, just like they used to do when one of them was going for a training, an interview or getting married. For this family, prestige was of utmost importance and they were disciplined into thinking that no price was too high if it bought them this prize. And now the father had decreed that each one come up with a sizeable sum towards the campaign fund to push the family oddball onto a seat in the Legislative Assembly.

So the stage was set for the big fight between the ruling-party heavyweight and the independent minnow. The new house that Nungsang had recently built became overnight a bustling hub of strange activities. People came in and out of it at all hours of the day and night. An amateur rock band suddenly appeared one morning pledging eternal support for the candidate and said that they would liven up the whole atmosphere with their music. They appropriated the empty space on the front verandah and set up their motley assortment of guitars and a drum set and a local garage owner lent his truck battery for the sound system to tide over the regular power cuts. From the word go they emitted loud shrieks and discordant sounds from their musical instruments, drowning out all other sounds, but everyone tolerated their efforts at making music in good humour. A makeshift kitchen suddenly sprang up in the backyard because Nungsang's wife refused to cook the big meals required for the ever-growing crowd of freeloaders. In this public kitchen, a distant cousin took charge of things. He was assisted by two hefty relatives: their size proving to be an effective deterrent to many of the rowdies, who after tasting the plentiful supply of free liquor in both the camps, would sometimes create havoc here. The public kitchen sometimes remained open way past midnight when the slightly tipsy cousin would signal to his muscle men to douse the roaring fire with buckets of water. The loud hissing of the dying embers was the signal that cousin-cook was retiring for the night.

The scenario in the house resembled a 'mela' gone haywire but, fortunately, there were no major mishaps. The canvassing, spearheaded by Bhandari and five other young contractors, was achieving the desired result: many young people and neutrals among the older generation were being converted to Nungsang's cause. The campaign, now stretching to almost a month, was doing well. But an unexpected event suddenly put a damper on the progress: four days before campaigning was to be over, the other camp took out a procession through the town, shouting slogans, beating drums and some were even seen taking swigs from bottles. The whole town came out to watch the seemingly endless vehicles carrying hundreds of supporters of the rival candidate. Nungsang's camp was caught unawares. The workers and supporters became disheartened by the sheer number of riders and their vociferous and very visible show of support to the other candidate. With no previous experience, nor new ideas about the ways of an election campaign, the chief agents were concentrating solely on meeting people in their homes and soliciting their votes for Nungsang, while the public kitcken took care of the general feeding of those avowed supporters who continued to flock to the open house. But Bhandari, the main organiser of the campaign, remained calm amidst the general gloom and set about countering whatever effects the opposition procession had had on the general public as well as their own workers. He decided that they, too, would take out a procession and immediately went to work: He called up his associates in town, who had trucks, and requested them to lend him the use of their vehicles for a procession the very next day. Even jeep owners were not spared.

Among the younger contractors was a boy called Imrong, who thought that their procession should do something different to wipe out whatever the previous procession might have accomplished. He went to Bhandari and explained his idea to him. The older man listened intently and immediately understood. But, he asked, what could be done in a few hours to achieve what Imrong proposed? Imrong replied that he required a few items: a large quantity of white long cloth, several dozen boxes of fabric paint, jute ropes and bamboo poles of specific sizes and lengths. Then he inducted a few of his friends into this group and declared that they would work all night to get the job done. But there was a rider; his group needed peace and quiet, so the band had to be dismissed by six in the evening. The self-styled musicians were not amused, but had to comply with the request of the main campaign agent and so, muttering obscenities under their breath, they reluctantly went home.

What Imrong planned was to paint symbols and slogans on the white cloth and decorate each truck with a number of these, while smaller pieces would be made into flags. All would carry Nungsang's election symbol: a beautiful hornbill. It seemed like an impossible task to accomplish in the few hours they had. But they had reckoned without Imrong's genius; he was a self-taught artist and had quite a reputation as an accomplished painter of signs and landscapes. The boys that he brought with him were all amateur artists. All night this dedicated band of painters worked under Imrong's instructions; from time to time Nungsang's wife brought them soup, tea, coffee and other savoury tid bits. From the public kitchen came a special dinner brought in by the two assistants. When they entered the room and saw what the boys had created, they almost dropped the trays of food, so awestruck were they by the beauty that lay before their eyes. They lovingly caressed the hornbills on the many flags and banners, murmuring to each other; 'so, this is what it looks like.' By the early hours of the morning, the house was strewn with the banners and flags hung up to dry with the image of the legendary bird beaming from every conceivable space. Anyone who entered the room instinctively felt that this symbol, so beautiful and life-like, was the harbinger of a new force which would rejuvenate the flagging spirits of the tired campaigners, especially after the 'coup' of the procession mounted by the opposition.

By early morning, Bhandari came in with his band of campaigners. When he saw what Imrong and his friends had accomplished overnight, he too, was awestruck. He knew then that the proposed procession would be the clincher and began to think of making it into a huge statement for the voting public. Then he recalled how the riders in the trucks had been seen drinking and behaving rowdily and decided that their procession would project a sober and civilized image instead. He called all the supporters and instructed them that mixed groups of old and young people must fill the vehicles during the rally and that they must all remain completely sober. No drunken and disorderly behaviour was going to be tolerated during the procession. For adding more grandeur, he persuaded a few of the elders to wear full traditional dress with headgear and in each truck made one such personage stand prominently as the centrepiece flanked by the younger people. Each vehicle would be packed to capacity. He and the other campaign organisers would ride in jeeps, which would follow the trucks. There would be no drum-beating or indiscriminate shouting: they would shout only 'vote for' at strategic locations and orchestrate them in such a way that the shouts would be relayed from the first vehicle to the last at ten-minute intervals.

As planned, the procession started from the compound at exactly 2 p.m. on a sunny afternoon, just forty-four hours before the end of campaigning. The trucks, all spruced up for the event, held orderly groups of young and old, bearing beautiful banners and flags. The pace was sedate and the shouts regular and well orchestrated. The townspeople, having witnessed the other show were at first puzzled; but as the procession made its way through the main streets of the town, more and more people came out to watch this new spectacle and stood rooted to their spots. They had never seen such disciplined behaviour. They remembered the other procession; the shrieks and the drunks hanging out of the vehicles, bottles in hand. There had been nothing beautiful in that earlier event.

After nearly two hours of orderly progression through the town, the triumphant procession returned to camp and had a rip-roaring party past midnight. Apart from the orderliness of human behaviour in the procession, what remained vivid in the minds of the townspeople was the mesmerizing sight of the magnificent birds fluttering from the banners and flags festooned on the slow-moving vehicles. Even years later, older people recalled that the sight of the legendary birds stirred something elemental in their racial memory and they fancied that the birds had descended from their lofty perches in the deep and dark jungles and had come to participate in the political parade with a clear message for the people. They claimed that their votes were swayed by the impact made by the sight of this ancestral symbol. It was indeed a fortuitous coincidence for Nungsang that he was allotted this symbol by the election office for he had had nothing to with it. But for many voters it was the defining factor in his favour rather than any new-fangled political ideology, which they did not understand anyway.

Election day came and as a precautionary measure, truckloads of casual labourers were brought from building and road construction sites as 'additional' voters who were instructed to put their signs on the hornbill. While they were waiting for their turn, one of them said aloud, 'Why do we have to put our signs only on the bird?' Immediately, someone from the line retorted, 'With this kind of money, drinks and a free meal, I would put my sign even on a snake if that was the instruction.' The group leader, who was all the time moving up and down the line to ensure that the boys behaved and did as they were told, heard the exchange and moved closer to the group. Lowering his voice, he spoke to them in their own language; 'Do as you have been instructed. Put your sign on the bird and only on the bird. If anyone disobeys, we will find out immediately and you know what will happen then.' Cautioning them to be quiet, he began his pacing once more. The labourers knew 'what would happen' if they did not do as instructed and stood meekly in their positions. When the turn of this bunch came, the Polling Officer suddenly got up from his seat and declared that he had to go to the toilet urgently and disappeared. His assistant, a young clerk temporarily inducted into the job, was quite nervous and forgot to scrutinize the slips of paper held by these outsiders in order to verify whether they were genuine voters or not, and allowed them to go inside the booths. All of them put their signs on the hornbill staring at them from the ballot paper. Afterwards they were taken to the public kitchen in the candidate's house, given liquor and food and the merry bunch then went back to their worksites richer by fifty rupees.

Counting day came amidst half-hearted claims and counter claims of irregularities, which, of course, were not entertained by the Returning Officer. When the final tally was taken, it was clear that Nungsang had won by a decent margin. After two days of more feasting and merry-making, the public kitchen was dismantled and the cousin and his bouncers were paid handsomely for their services. The musicians packed their frayed instruments and after haggling over their rewards, went home, still grumbling about some people's insensitivity to good music and their miserliness. Imrong, the creator of the beautiful birds won praise from many people, even from some in the rival camp who said that it was the bird that won the votes for Nungsang. But from the winner, Imrong got only a vague promise of distant rewards, which was of course promptly forgotten. For Bhandari and his select coterie, the rewards for their contribution would come later, in many different ways. Bhandari was willing to wait; he would demand his 'pound of flesh' at the appropriate moment. He would press the new Legislator to spearhead the introduction of a bill to recognise his tribe as an indigenous group in the state.

The next evening, the select group led by Bhandari came to the new M.L.A.'s house for a celebratory party. But by then fatigue had set in and both guests and hosts were beginning to feel the effects of the hectic campaign, which had just ended. They were in no mood for a prolonged party. After a few drinks, they went off, leaving Nungsang and his wife with a few hangers-on. Unlike other nights, everyone dispersed by eleven o'clock and the house too seemed to shut itself down. The sudden silence after the noise and confusion of earlier nights seemed to create an air of unreality all round and without saying much to each other, the M.L.A. and his wife went to bed.

Nungsang's term as a contractor was coming to an end and he gave Bhandari the power-of-attorney so that he could wind up the business on his behalf. Thus ended a chapter in the life of the man who, in search of an identity, had gone into business because it was the only course left to a person with his credentials. This new venture, too, was undertaken with the same purpose. The whirlwind campaign and the ease with which he seemed to have made the transition impressed many observers. But little did they know of the many casualties he had left by the roadside on his way to the House. The moment his candidature was announced, his sub-contractors began to fear the worst: at the best of times they never got full payments, and now if he got elected, they could forget all their pending bills. And after the results were declared, their fears were confirmed and they sadly closed that chapter in their 'khatas'. But what really galled them was the fact that they had to give, not donations but subscriptions, on the directive of the Contractors' Union, to the campaign fund of the man who had strung them along on false assurances for years. Being shrewd businessmen however, they recognised the importance of this emerging group as the new force in the power structure of the state and with an eye to their own survival they complied without a murmur. So the Abdul Sattars, Karims and many other petty suppliers of the market were left licking their wounds while the newly elected Member made preparations to go to Kohima for the oath taking and formal induction to the House.

For Merenla of the pumpkins, it was quite another story. Ever since she had entered into an agreement with Nungsang to supply him as many pumpkins as she could grow, she had planted only this crop in much of her field season after season. The villagers

were amused at first, but when they saw her doing this year after
year and earning good money for her efforts, they began to call
her pumpkin Merenla. In the beginning, this soubriquet did not
bother her; she rather liked it because the pumpkins were indeed
bringing her good money. But from the moment she heard that
Nungsang was aiming for higher things in life, she had begun to
worry, for unlike other years, this season, she not only planted
pumpkin seeds in her own field but she even leased a portion of
her neighbour's land to do the same. By the time the election
result was known, Merenla's pumpkins were rapidly turning from
green to yellow in the process of maturing. Whether she had a
buyer or not, she had to harvest the lot and with grave foreboding
she gathered them with the help of her sons. As usual, they were
to be stacked on the bamboo platform at the back of the house
but because of the additional harvest, the space on the platform
fell short. So some pumpkins had to be stacked on top of the
woodpile as well. Merenla still hoped that Nungsang would not
abandon her with this surplus crop and that he would help her
somehow. She had heard that his friend Bhandari was looking
after his business now and maybe, just maybe, Nungsang would
instruct him to relieve the poor woman of her harvest, which was
very likely going to become a 'burden' for her if no buyer turned
up. But there was no word from either Nungsang or his friend.
This poor woman who had innocently believed that she had
found an easier way of earning a livelihood through this
arrangement with her cousin, now found herself totally abandoned.
She felt quite betrayed. In all these years she never knew what role
her pumpkins played in her cousin's unscrupulous scramble for
money and power and how she had been used in his scheme of
dark dealings. All that she knew was that she had to earn a living
for her sons and herself, and she had thought that she had
stumbled on a good and honest way by collaborating with her
cousin. But the man who opened this doorway for her, seemed
to be totally unconcerned about her fate now that he had
ascended a higher road. This, she thought, was cruel because she
was brought up on the tradition that family ties were more

sacrosanct than any others and besides, he did have a business obligation to her as well. Slowly and painfully she began to see that people who go away from villages think and act differently even if they are relatives. She said to herself over and over again that a fellow villager would never have treated her in this manner.

Days went by and no one came for her pumpkins. Now when she heard herself addressed as pumpkin Merenla, she would flare up and scream at the person who addressed her thus. She became irritable with her sons and they began to spend more time outside than at home, which further incensed the poor harassed woman. Nature, too, seemed to be turning against her: some of her pumpkins were ripening too fast and rotting in the stacks. The house was beginning to stink horribly because of this. Beset by this cruel turn of events, Merenla stopped going out and spent most of her time lying on her cot. Her sister-in-law came one day and asked her if she could take some of the pumpkins to feed her pigs. She said yes listlessly and remembered her prize sow which was 'stolen' by the so and so's from the underground; she thought that if she had some pigs, she could have at least fed them some portion of the harvest, which was now 'infesting' her house as well as her mind. Lying in bed she thought long and hard and saw that it was her naivete and blind trust in her cousin that had landed her in this predicament. Deep in her heart she knew that she had to do something about it but a crippling lethargy seemed to overwhelm her and she lay there for days staring at nothing. Far greater than the financial loss was the 'loss of face' suffered by the widow in the community because of her cousin's heartlessness and it was this which hurt her the most. But as a mother she had to think of her sons and eventually the lost look on their faces and the suffocating stench of the rotting pumpkins galvanized her into action. She said to herself that she could not continue in this manner forever and that life had to somehow go on. The next morning she got up from the cot with a new determination and called her sons to help her sort out the good pumpkins from the rotten ones. Then she instructed them to inform all the relatives to come and take as many of them as they wanted. The rotten ones she set aside on the platform. Many of her once-prized pumpkins thus became distress gifts to families, who converted them to pig food when they themselves grew tired of eating pumpkin curry at every meal. And yet many more remained, threatening once more to engulf Merenla and her sons with their rotting odour symbolising the great debacle of this simple woman's venture as a 'supplier'. So one fine morning she decided to close this chapter of her life by doing something spectacular.

She sent off her sons to their uncle's field quite early in the morning. Choosing the moment when she knew that all the villagers would be on their way to the far-flung fields, Merenla proceeded with her plan. She left the front door wide open so that people could see right through to the platform at the back, where she would be performing. Wearing a red scarf on her head, Merenla began to shout 'Vote For' loudly and with every shout she would hurl a pumpkin to the ground below. The initial shouts went unheard, but when the village pigs began to scramble for the shattered pieces of the pumpkins with loud squeals and grunts, the noise attracted the attention of the people going to their fields. They stopped to investigate; some even entered the house to find this quiet woman hurling her produce as though she was performing a strange ritual to get rid of something 'unclean' as in the old days. Unaffected by the presence of her fellow villagers Merenla continued. She silently welcomed their presence because they had unwittingly become witnesses to her performance.

There was something essentially childlike in a grown woman taking out her frustration on some common vegetables and yet, those who saw the scene on the bamboo platform came away with a distinct impression that the simple act of throwing out the pumpkins signified a deep resolve in the mind of this poor widow to reorganise her life. The ludicrous performance did not in any way diminish the inherent pathos of her situation. The spectators were deeply moved, but they did not say anything, either to her or to fellow villagers, who had witnessed the frenzied performance. They merely shook their heads and went on their way.

When she got tired, Merenla stopped to eat her mid-day meal and rested for a while. The platform was by now cleared but there were still quite a few pumpkins left in the woodpile. Tired as she was, she was determined to rid her home and her life of all the reminders of her earlier association with her kinsman, and as soon as she felt rested, she resumed the task of 'cleansing'. The pigs lolling on the ground below the platform had gorged themselves on the windfall so much that they ignored the loud thuds now, which had attracted them in the first place and did not even look at the pink juicy bits lying all around them. But undeterred by their indifference, Merenla continued her exercise and by late afternoon had finished destroying all the fruit of her hard labour. Exhausted, she swept the entire house, including the outer room where wood was piled. She then lit a huge fire, heated water and had a long, leisurely bath. When the sons came back in the evening from their uncle's farm where they had gone to work for a wage, they were pleasantly surprised to see their mother looking somehow different in her Sunday clothes. The house, too, was swept and all spruced up. There was not a single pumpkin in sight. They also noticed that she was in a cheerful mood; gone was the despondency and lethargy of the previous days. Though young, they instinctively realised that their mother had got a fresh lease of life and felt greatly comforted as if she had actually hugged and held them close to her bosom.

Simple village folk have a unique and singular way of using language, therefore calling the widow 'pumpkin Merenla' was their way of adding a new dimension to her identity during the period of her association with Nungsang, the contractor. There was no malice or ridicule intended in the sobriquet. In the very same way, long ago a villager named Longritoba brought the seeds of the tomato plant to the village to find out if it could be grown here. He discovered that it did well in the village, and by the second year he was able to supply seedlings to whoever wanted them. This vegetable became very popular and automatically came to be called 'Longritoba *pendu*', meaning, 'Longritoba's tomato' because it was he who had first introduced it to the village. So was the case with pumpkin Merenla. But now under the altered circumstances, the villagers recognised the message that she conveyed to them through her very vociferous and public rejection of this identity on the day that she had 'cleansed' her house and herself of something that had 'wounded' her both in the material and psychological sense.

From that day on, in acknowledgement of her symbolic act, and out of sympathy for a fellow villager, no one in the village ever used the sobriquet once attached to her name. Life in the village went on as before and this simple woman, now called Merenla as before, unobtrusively merged into the rhythm of age-old village life, far away from the political permutations and combinations forming and re-forming elsewhere in the land.